TRAVELING CIRCUS
AND THE
SECRET TALENT
SCROLL

Story and Illustrations by

Ingar Rudholm

INGAR RUPHOL

ISBN: 1-944815-78-3
ISBN13: 978-1-944815-78-3

Dedications

To: Lilli C. and Lilly W.
Your words of encouragement cut through
my self-doubt and gave me the courage
to complete this book...thank-you!

Acknowledgements

Co-written and Edited by Kelsey Turek

A special thanks to Donald Ingersoll
for your continued support.

1

~

Cordelia grinned from ear to ear and her heart pounded with joy; she barely contained her excitement. The letter was a dream come true. She read it over again to make sure it was real.

Ms. Cordelia Da Vinci,

Ninety athletes have been invited to participate in the final phase of "Scouting Camp: Potential Olympic Athletes," which will be held at the Delta Training and Swim Center in Grand Rapids, MI on September 7. The U.S. talent program aims to build a pipeline of world-class athletes pursuing an Olympic dream. Nearly 2,000 individuals submitted applications and we chose you to participate.

We hope to see you soon and good luck!

Sincerely,
Official Swim Team Committee

This could change my life, Cordelia thought as she carefully folded the letter and placed it back into her pocket.

Cordelia was on the last weekend of summer vacation before returning to high school for her senior year.

Her father, Salvatore, drove them along the back roads of West Michigan. He twirled his thin, black mustache in half circles with his finger. His black hair remained frozen in place with thick gel and his skin paled in comparison with his wife's tanned complexion.

Cordelia's mother, Gala, sat in the passenger's seat making a lace doily. She could've been Cordelia's twin sister—she had the same red hair, green eyes, and soft cheek bones.

Her dad's rusty old car hit a bump in the road, causing the metal frame to rattle. Cordelia wished they had a nicer car, but money was tight. Feeling warm, she rolled down the window and the wind blew through her long curly hair. A streak of green oak leaves whizzed past her window as she inhaled the fresh air.

They entered Whitehall, a small town filled with retail shops that resembled old-time photos. As they reached the far edge of town, her father turned left on a road that followed along White Lake's shore. A few boats sailed on the choppy water toward a manmade channel that fed into Lake Michigan. A lighthouse that guided ships through the White Lake channel for over one hundred years appeared above the tree line.

Her father pulled into a driveway with a sign that read "L.C. Woodruff Inn". A weathered brick exterior and a steep gable roof made the old building look tall. A picture window accentuated the front and a large bay window was centered on the west wall, providing a great view in all directions.

The wood steps creaked as they climbed to the front porch. Her father opened the heavy varnished door for Cordelia and her mom.

"Ladies first," he said with a wink and nod.

A grand staircase sat in the center of the foyer, leading up to the bedrooms. To the left was a small gift shop with souvenirs. To the right, an elderly lady stood behind a check-in counter. With rimmed glasses and grey hair, she looked at home with an old-fashioned cash register.

While her parents checked in, Cordelia meandered over to the gift shop. A display rack with photography books caught her attention. Picking the one with a shipwreck on the cover, she flipped it over and read the description.

"During a strong stormy night, the *L.C. Woodruff* capsized and sank near the White Lake Channel after World War II. The ferry boat still remains hidden at the bottom of Lake Michigan."

Returning the book, she glanced over at a miniature pirate ship with tiny ropes and sails. She reached out her hand and touched one of the masts.

A gruff male's voice with a strong Russian accent shouted, "Don't touch that!"

The hairs on the back of her neck bristled as she spun around and saw a wrinkly old man snarling at her. He had yellow teeth and a scraggly beard.

"You break it, you buy it," he growled. His narrowed eyes stared at her.

Frightened by his demeanor, Cordelia scampered back to her father's side.

The lady behind the counter, whose name tag read "Mrs. Rusalka," said, "Viktor is grumpy today. Luckily you didn't stay here last night."

"Really; why?" Salvatore asked.

"We had a bad thunderstorm and lost power," Mrs. Rusalka rambled. "Heavy winds knocked down trees, and huge waves pushed sand onto the beach. I don't even recognize the shoreline anymore."

Gala's eyes widened. "Wow."

Mrs. Rusalka held up a key. "You're in room seven, upstairs. Enjoy your stay."

"Thank you," Salvatore said, taking the key.

Cordelia carried her suitcase upstairs and followed her parents down a long hallway with numbered doors. Her dad stopped at door seven and opened it. The large room contained a fireplace, a picture window, and a king-size bed. A doorway on the opposite wall led to a second small bedroom for Cordelia. She walked over to her room, set her suitcase on the bed, and opened it.

"Can I go to the beach?" Cordelia asked. She couldn't wait to dip her feet into Lake Michigan.

"Yes, but I want to give you something first." Her mother reached into her bag and held up a green bathing suit. "I made it for your swim competition, but you might as well try it out now."

Excited, Cordelia ran into the bathroom and tried it on. Her mother was an excellent seamstress and she made all of Cordelia's clothes. As always, it fit perfectly.

"Thanks, Mom!" she showed off her new suit.

"You're welcome, sweetie."

"Mom, where did you learn to sew clothes?" Cordelia asked.

"Well," Gala looked lovingly at her husband. "That's a great question. It's kinda what brought your dad and me together."

"Really? Tell me more," Cordelia said; she smiled and sat on the edge of the bed.

"When I was your age, I dreamed of becoming a costume designer," Gala said. "I had money set aside for college, but that wasn't enough for my books. On my summer break, I looked in the newspaper for a part-time job. I found an ad looking for someone to make costumes for your Grandpa Albert's traveling circus."

Twisting his mustache, Salvatore sat down next to Cordelia. "And I worked as the ringmaster during the day, and I attended community college at night."

"Your grandpa bought an old sewing machine and fabric," Gala continued. "He wanted me to create a ringmaster's outfit for your dad."

"You made Dad's suit?" Cordelia asked.

Gala nodded.

"When I stepped into the dressing room to get fitted, I was blown away by your mom's beauty," Salvatore said with a glimmer in his eye. "I couldn't take my eyes off her."

"I was so nervous taking his measurements," Gala added. "I almost dropped the sewing tape."

Cordelia chuckled, looking up at her dad.

"I couldn't let her get away," Salvatore said, rubbing Cordelia's back. "Before your mom went back to college, I asked for her address and we wrote letters back and forth."

"Aw, that's so sweet," Cordelia sighed.

"After college, I went to work for your grandpa full-time," Gala said. "Your father asked me to marry him, and the rest is history."

Cordelia smiled at the end of the story. She always wondered about the full story of how her parents met.

4

Salvatore stood up, walked over to Gala, and kissed her on the cheek. "Marrying you was the best decision I've ever made."

~

The sun-bleached sand felt coarse on Cordelia's heels and toes, sending shivers down her spine. It sounded like corduroy jeans brushing together as she walked along the dunes. Waves crashed on the shore, and the seagulls squawked as they circled overhead. She crested the top of the hill eroded by the storm. Driftwood and rocks were scattered along the beach. Her pupils contracted when she gazed upon the clear blue skies and the sun reflecting off the rolling waves of Lake Michigan.

With the wind blowing through her hair, she dropped her towel on the beach, ran toward the lake, and dove into the refreshing water. She swam about fifty feet from the shore until her feet touched a ridge of sand created by the movement of the waves. At the bottom of a steep decline, a long black object lay below the surface. It was larger than a whale—over a hundred feet long.

What is that? she wondered.

Her swim coach had taught her how to hold her breath for over two minutes, which would give her time to investigate the object. She dove underwater and swam toward the eerie shadow.

Through blurry eyes, she found a sunken ferry boat tilted on an angle, half-buried in the sand. The words *L.C. Woodruff* were written on the side! Swimming closer, she saw the guardrail covered with green algae and corroded with age. A gaping hole went through the main deck and out the bottom of the ship as if it had been struck by a missile. She peered inside the hole. Sand filled the interior of the ship and a human skeleton clutching a green metal box floated with the current; both leg bones were broken and the skull was cracked open.

Frightened, she propelled her body back to the surface and floated on her back for a few minutes, catching her breath and calming her nerves.

What's inside in the box and why would someone die protecting it? she wondered.

Curiosity overcame her fears. Taking a deep breath, she dove back underwater.

Avoiding the jagged metal, she entered the hole in the ship. She swam to the skeleton and tugged on the box, breaking it free from the boney hands. She tucked the box under one arm and, kicking with her legs, shot to the water's surface like a rocket and swam toward the beach.

A wave crashed over her head. Water poured into her throat and burned her lungs. Even though she was a strong swimmer, her muscles struggled against the current. Disoriented, she couldn't breathe. Bubbles floated out of her mouth. Her muscles were sore and the box became an anchor. The undertow tugged at her legs, pulling her to the bottom of the big lake.

2

A strong arm grabbed Cordelia by the waist and pulled her to the surface. She coughed up water as the old man from the gift shop dragged her to the shore. When they reached the beach, they both collapsed from exhaustion. The sun drained all of the energy out her aching muscles. She laid her head on the sand and closed her eyes as she tried to catch her breath.

~

The crunching sound of breaking metal jolted her awake. The old man broke the rusty latch on the container with a large rock. He opened the water-tight seal with a pocket knife and rummaged through the box.

She tried to speak, but her throat was dry. The sun's glaring rays made her head dizzy. Someone was running down the beach toward them. Was it Dad?

As Salvatore approached, he asked, slightly out of breath, "What's going on?"

Feeling relieved to see her father, Cordelia propped herself up on her elbows, pointed to the box, and explained, "I found it in the lake."

Salvatore stood in front of Viktor with his arms crossed, shielding Cordelia.

"That's my property," the old man claimed, puffing out his

chest.

"Well, Lake Michigan isn't on your property," Salvatore said, picking up the box. "Do you have proof it belongs to you?"

The old man shook his head and stormed off, muttering under his breath, "Nobody treats me this way. If only I were thirty years younger."

Salvatore glared at the old man as he disappeared over the dunes. Offering his hand to Cordelia, he helped her stand up. She felt secure knowing her dad was there to protect her.

"Did he hurt you?" her dad asked. "Are you okay?"

"No, I'm not hurt," Cordelia responded. "He rescued me from the undertow."

Looking at the box, Salvatore said, "Wait a minute. This is an ammo box. This could be very dangerous."

"I didn't know," Cordelia replied.

"You need to be more careful," Salvatore added with concern in his voice.

"Okay, I will," Cordelia promised.

"What's inside?"

"It's empty, except for these," her dad said, pulling out a scroll and a skeleton key.

"Can I keep it?" she asked. "They're kinda neat."

Her dad sighed. "Sure. But how did you find it?"

Cordelia hesitated; she didn't want him to change his mind about keeping it.

"When I went swimming in the lake, I found the box inside a sunken ship. The boat was *L.C. Woodruff*!"

Her dad's eyes widened. "Really? Cordelia, that was dangerous. You could've been hurt or drowned!"

"I'm sorry," she replied, feeling ashamed that she let her father down. She knew her dad loved and cared about her.

He wrapped his arm around her shoulder. "Be more careful, okay?"

She nodded as they walked back to the Inn.

~

As thunder rumbled across the hot August night sky, Cordelia lay in bed thinking about what she had found. A flash of lightning followed by a thunderclap shook the walls. Raindrops splashed against the window while her dad snored in the other room.

She quietly slid out of bed, turned on a lamp, and tiptoed over to the ammo box. The hinges creaked as she pried it open. She looked toward her parents, hoping she didn't wake them.

The box smelled like old dust, and the interior looked dry. She reached inside and pulled out the skeleton key and the scroll with the words "Secret Talent Scroll" written on the side. She silently read the words on the tattered and worn paper:

Everyone has a natural talent, whether language, music, arts, or science. Use the spell on the scroll to turn your talents into extraordinary powers! Find something that represents your talent and read the spell out loud to receive the desired power.

"I call upon the four classical elements: wind, fire, earth, and water. Wind moves sand. Fire creates earth and ash. Earth absorbs water. Water quenches fire." Say the person's name and their desired power.

If the person uses the power for evil, the spell can be broken with this chant:

"I call upon the four classical elements: wind, fire, earth, and water. Wind moves sand. Fire creates earth and ash. Earth absorbs water. Water quenches fire." Say the person's name and remove their desired power.

Hearing her father stir in the other room, she placed the scroll and key back inside the box, turned off the lamp, and hopped into bed.

What does the key open? Maybe I can use the scroll to win the Olympics? she wondered as her eyelids became heavy and her mind drifted into a deep sleep.

3

~

The morning light sifted through the venetian blinds. Cordelia looked down at the foot of the bed and noticed the box was missing. In panic, she jumped out of bed and stormed into the next room.

"Mom, the old man stole the box!"

"Calm down, your dad took it to the car already."

Cordelia sighed with relief.

"Pack your suitcase and get dressed. We're going downstairs for breakfast."

"Can we stay a little longer?" Cordelia asked while her stomach growled. "I want to go for another swim."

"No. Your father and I want to celebrate our anniversary alone. You can stay behind with your grandpa and keep him out of trouble at the circus." Her mom chuckled.

~

After checking out of the Inn, Salvatore drove into town. In the back seat, Cordelia opened up the ammo container and pulled out the skeleton key. It was about four inches long and the top had an oval ring with a lightning bolt in the center.

I'll show it to my grandpa later. Maybe he can tell me more about it, she thought, stuffing the key into her front pocket.

A silver streak flashed in the side passenger mirror, catching

Cordelia's eye. She turned around and looked out the rear window. The old man from the gift shop was driving in his car behind them. Her stomach clenched, and her fingernails dug into the seat cushions.

"Dad!" Cordelia exclaimed. "That creepy old man is back."

"Oh no," Gala said, her shoulders tensed.

The vehicle turned down a side street.

Glancing in the rear-view mirror, Salvatore said in a reassuring voice, "See, he's not following us. There's nothing to worry about. You're safe."

"Should we call the police?" Gala asked.

"He hasn't done anything," Salvatore replied. "We'll be all right." He rubbed her shoulder.

Salvatore drove into the parking lot of Funnell Field and parked. Cordelia grabbed her duffle bag and the ammo box.

The smell of roasted peanuts and popcorn drifted through the air. A giant circus tent stood in the middle of the field. The sideshow tents lined the left side of the park, and the carnival rides were on the right.

Cordelia's grandfather, Albert, owned a traveling circus and carnival. During the summer, they toured all over Michigan, setting up shows in city parks. After a few days, they would tear down the equipment and move to a different town. Her dad was the ringmaster of the circus, Cordelia helped her mom sew costumes for the performers, and her grandpa's stage name was Albert the Fortune Teller. During the winter, Cordelia and her mom would stay in a cabin in Siren Bay, Michigan, so she could attend school and swim practice while her dad and grandpa traveled south with the circus. She always missed her dad and grandpa when they were gone.

They strolled by a Ferris Wheel, a rickety old roller coaster, and a Tilt-A-Whirl. When they found Albert's RV on the back side of Funnell Field, Cordelia set her duffle bag and the ammo box down on the ground. Salvatore knocked on the door.

After no one answered, Salvatore turned to Cordelia. "He must be in his tent."

~

With the help of a flickering candle on a table, Cordelia's eyes slowly adjusted to the dark tent. The walls had green and red stripes, and the ceiling had been painted to look like the sky. A crystal ball sat on a table in the middle of the room. She knew the crystal ball didn't work, but everyone came to Albert the Fortune Teller's tent because he always gave good advice.

A gravelly voice spoke from behind a star-covered curtain on the back wall, "Please have a seat."

"We're home," Salvatore replied.

The curtain slid open to reveal her Grandpa Albert. He had untamed hair, a gray bushy mustache, and a face full of wrinkles. His hooded robe draped from his shoulders to his toes. Skin crinkled around his eyes as he walked over to Cordelia and gave her a warm hug.

"Can you watch Cordelia for a few days while we go away for our anniversary?" Salvatore asked.

Albert nodded. "I'll be the ringmaster until you return."

Gala handed Albert a lace doily that she had made for him and said, "I thought you could put it under your crystal ball."

"Thank you," Albert said with a wink. "By the way, I bought an anniversary present for the both of you."

He reached into his pocket and pulled out a small gift box.

Gala's face lit up as she unwrapped a gold pocket watch with a long chain and their wedding date engraved on the back.

Gala gave Albert a hug and thanked him for the gift.

Salvatore looked over at Cordelia and said, "Could you give us a few minutes. I need to talk to your grandpa alone."

She nodded, stepped outside the tent, and looked around. Parents stood by the security fence while their kids rode carnival rides. Screams of excitement and laughter echoed through the park. She knew this made her Grandpa Albert happy.

All the activities distracted her for a moment when suddenly she heard her father raise his voice in frustration.

I wonder what they're talking about? she thought.

She stepped closer to the tent, tilted her head sideways, and listened to their conversation.

"I need money for our vacation," Salvatore grumbled.

"What happened to the extra money I gave you last week?" Albert responded.

"I spent it on groceries and car repairs."

"Now you want money for fun things, too?" Albert asked with irritation. "Son, nothing in life is free."

"If the circus made money, you could pay me more," Salvatore complained. "Then I could support my family."

Cordelia bit her bottom lip. Hearing them argue about money made her feel uncomfortable.

"You should've finished your degree in physics instead of dropping out of college," Albert said. "You would've made more money as a scientist.

"I was failing my classes! Besides, I needed a job to support my family. You're the one who wanted me to go to college. That's not what I wanted."

"You should've applied yourself more!" Albert shot back. "You had so much talent."

The conversation went silent, and Salvatore shuffled his feet.

"I don't need to be treated like a child," Salvatore muttered under his breath as he stormed out of the tent.

Salvatore marched across the field, jumped into the driver's seat of his car, and stared out the windshield. Cordelia's mom and grandpa emerged from the tent.

"Thanks for giving us extra money when we need it," Gala said, squeezing Albert's hand. "I know he struggled in college."

Albert let out a long sigh.

Life would be different if my dad hadn't dropped out of college, Cordelia thought. *They wouldn't be arguing so much.*

"Fortunately, you gave him a job to fall back on," Gala continued.

"I'll try to go easy on him from now on," Albert said, letting out a sigh.

"Thank you," Gala softly replied.

Gala walked over to Cordelia, kissed her forehead, and said goodbye. As she walked away, Cordelia noticed a wad of cash in her mother's hand.

As her parents drove off, Albert walked over to Cordelia, placed his hand on her shoulder, and gently squeezed it. She looked up at him, still a little rattled by her father's sudden departure.

"Things are going to be okay," Albert said reassuringly. "Your dad will get over it."

Cordelia wearily nodded.

"Change into your bathing suit, and grab a towel," Albert insisted with a smirk. "I want to show you something."

She smiled; she loved surprises.

~

Ropes and poles propped up the brown canvas roof of the main circus tent. A chain of overhead lights shone down on three circular stages. In the center ring, Paula and Rego practiced on the trapeze equipment while two trained white doves synchronized with their act. A high diving board and an above-ground swimming pool sat next to the center ring. The diving board stood 30 feet in the air, nearly touching the roof of the tent.

"I bought this for you," Albert explained, pointing to the diving board. "I know how you love to swim. You found your life's purpose as a swimmer."

His words warmed her heart and made her smile.

"Instead of making costumes, maybe someday you'll be a part of the circus act too?" Albert asked, raising his eyebrows. "I figured you could try it out and see if you like it."

Cordelia felt a tinge of guilt. She never told her grandpa that she didn't want to stay with the circus. She was afraid of hurting his feelings. After watching the summer Olympics on TV, she dreamed of being on the U.S. Swim Team. At six years old, her training began at the local YMCA. Her instructor trained her in several techniques, including the freestyle, backstroke, and springboard diving. All her hard work paid off when she joined the swim team in high school.

"Thanks, Grandpa!" she said and gave him a hug.

"You're welcome. I need to get ready for our performance. I'll be back later. Why don't you check out your diving board?"

"Sure," Cordelia said.

As Albert walked out of the tent, Paula and Rego finished practicing their routine and climbed down the trapeze ladder.

"Hey!" Paula said, undoing her long blonde hair from a ponytail. The white dove landed on her shoulder as she approached Cordelia. "You're back. How was your vacation?"

"Pretty good," Cordelia responded. "I went swimming in Lake Michigan and I found a sunken ship."

"Really?" Paula asked. "That's pretty cool."

"I also met this creepy old man," Cordelia said. "He freaked me out."

Rego flexed his tan muscles and tossed his dove in the air. The bird performed a few back flips, fluttered in the air, and landed on his shoulder.

"Did he hurt you?" Rego asked as his bushy brown mustache twitched. Paula and Rego acted like protective older siblings, even though they weren't family.

Cordelia shivered. "No, but I hope I never see him again."

"If he does come around here, I'll take care of him," Rego grunted.

"So, are you going to show us your moves on the diving board?" Paula asked. "I heard you're multitalented, both an excellent swimmer and diver."

Blushing, Cordelia said, "Yeah, I can show you a few things."

Cordelia walked over to the pool and climbed the ladder to the diving board. When she reached the top, she breathed in deeply and focused her mind on all the training from her coach. She took three quick steps and leaped high into the air. Keeping her body in a straight line, she rolled her hips forward creating a flat back.

WHOOSH!

She entered the water creating a small ripple without making a splash.

Popping her head above the water, she heard Paula and Rego clapping. She swam over to the lip of the pool and leaned over the side as a smile spread across her face.

"Good job!" Rego said.

Before Cordelia could respond, her hair bristled on the back of her neck as the old man from the L.C. Woodruff Inn walked into the tent with her grandpa.

4

~

"Cordelia, could I talk to you for a minute?" Albert firmly asked.

Goosebumps covered her skin and her body trembled as she climbed out of the pool. She quickly dried off with a towel and put on her t-shirt.

"This man told me you stole his property. Is that true?" Albert asked.

"I found an ammo box in Lake Michigan. Dad said I could keep it."

Albert scowled at the old man and demanded, "Is that true?"

"Yes, but it was near my property," the man responded, tapping his briefcase. "I'm willing to pay a lot of money for it."

"That doesn't make any sense," Albert replied. "My granddaughter finds something in a public lake and now you want to buy it from her? What's so special about it, and why should we sell it to you?"

"Okay, I'll tell you the truth," the old man said. "My name is Viktor Rusalka. During World War II, I belonged to Russia's Red Army. My fellow comrade Ivan and I stormed Hitler's private bunker in Germany and confiscated hundreds of artifacts, including a scroll with a magic spell on it. I truly believed Hitler used its magic to gain control over Germany and then tried taking over the world. I showed it to my commanding officers, but they just laughed at me."

Cordelia crossed her arms and rolled her eyes.

"Why would you tell us this nonsense?" Albert asked, raising his eyebrows.

"I'm here to warn you. Please, let me finish. I will explain."

"Okay," Albert reluctantly agreed, pointing to his watch. "But you only have a few minutes because I have a business to run."

"I understand," Viktor continued. "I hid the scroll in an ammo box. After the war, I returned home and became an electrician. My friend Ivan and I came up with this crazy idea to use the scroll's magic to harness the power of a lightning bolt. We could make millions by lighting up cities. Russia was in chaos, so Ivan and I fled to America to pursue the dream. We settled in Michigan because I had relatives who lived here. One afternoon, I read an article in the paper that they were building an electrical power plant in Oak Creek, Wisconsin. Ivan and I saved our money and purchased two tickets on the *L.C. Woodruff*. As the ferry boat passed through the White Lake Channel late at night, we went on the ship's deck to see if the scroll really worked. All the other passengers were below because it had started to rain. Ivan opened up the ammo box and gave me the scroll. I brought a skeleton key that would be the object representing my talent. I read the chant, and the tip of the key glowed bright orange. The boat hit some rocky waves and my arm wavered. A giant lightning bolt sprang from the tip of the key and blew a hole in the deck and down through the hull of the ship. Fearing for my life, I threw the scroll and key back into the box. The ship filled with water and turned sideways. I grabbed onto the guardrail, but Ivan refused to let go of the ammo box. He fell into the hole created by the lightning bolt. I tried to save him but a wave knocked me overboard."

Cordelia shook her head in disbelief.

"I never saw my friend again," Viktor continued, wiping away a tear. "Like a good soldier, I stayed in Michigan and guarded the scroll and key. It could be dangerous if they fall into the wrong hands. I learned the hard way to be careful what you wish for."

"How come you didn't use it in Russia?" Albert asked, letting out a sigh.

"The government would steal my idea. America is a land of

opportunity, no?"

"Yes, it is," Albert replied.

"After the terrible storm the other night, the waves must've washed away the sand and uncovered the *L.C. Woodruff*. That's how your granddaughter found the ammo box."

"That's a pretty wild story," Albert replied.

"I speak the truth!" Viktor exclaimed, puffing out his chest.

Viktor set the briefcase on the ground and opened it. Cordelia's heart began to race when she saw piles of cash inside.

"How much do you want for the scroll and key?" Viktor asked. "I can offer you twenty-thousand dollars. Does that sound fair?"

Albert looked at Cordelia and said, "You found the scroll. Do you want to keep it or sell it?"

"Thirty-thousand," Viktor said, puffing out his chest.

Dollar signs flashed through Cordelia's head, but the scroll remained a mystery to her.

Is Viktor's story true? she wondered. *Should I take the deal? If the scroll is magic, it's worth more than money...*

"No," she blurted out.

"I don't want to take the scroll from you. I'd rather purchase it," Viktor stated gruffly.

"I'm sorry, Viktor, but I don't like your tone or threats. Please leave," Albert said pointing toward the tent entrance.

"You're making a big mistake," Viktor protested.

"If you don't leave now, I'm calling the cops," Albert threatened.

Rego, who overheard the whole conversation, stepped in and crossed his muscular arms.

"You heard Albert; go!" Rego grunted.

Viktor closed the briefcase and picked it up. He hobbled out the main entrance of the tent, grumbling under his breath.

"Grandpa," Cordelia said. "I'm scared he'll be back."

"Don't worry," Albert replied, patting her on the shoulder. "I'll go to the police and talk to them."

Cordelia relaxed a little bit.

"Where's the ammo box?" Albert asked. "I'll take it to the

police. They'll know what to do."

"I left it by your camper," she responded.

"Okay, I'll go get it."

"Can I go with you?" she asked.

"No, stay here with Rego," Albert said reassuringly. "He'll protect you."

"Yes I will," Rego agreed, flexing his muscles.

Cordelia cracked a smile.

~

I wonder what the police will do? Cordelia thought.

An hour had passed since she had seen her grandpa, and she worried Viktor would be back for the scroll.

As the circus performers prepared for the show, Cordelia carried her luggage to her parents' camper. A smile spread across her face when she saw her three white rabbits hopping around inside their cage next to the RV. She opened the door and picked them up. They wiggled their tails and tickled her arms with their whiskers. Setting them on the ground, she sprinkled food pellets on the dirt and they began to eat their dinner.

One of them escaped and hopped into a clump of trees. She scooped up the other two rabbits and locked them back in their cage.

"Nixie, come back here!" Cordelia pleaded, chasing after the wayward rabbit.

The bunny scurried into a giant foxhole in a mound of dirt.

Oh no, she's going to be eaten!

Cordelia cautiously approached the dark hole and sprinkled more food pellets on the ground. Hearing a scratching sound, she nervously peered inside the hole. Glowing red eyes glared back at her. Startled, she stepped away. After a few moments, the rabbit crawled out of the hole, covered in dirt. Letting out a sigh of relief, she scolded the rabbit as she carried it back to the cage.

Cordelia stepped inside her parent's camper and unpacked her luggage. As she changed out of her swimsuit, she felt a bulge in the pocket of her pants. She reached in and pulled out the skeleton key.

Suddenly, she heard a ruckus outside, and the camper door burst open. She screamed and her heart thumped in her chest when she saw Rego on the ground holding his head. She panicked and stood frozen in fear as two men entered the room. One was tall and skinny with long black hair and tattoos covering his arms. The other, a stocky man carrying a pistol, had short hair and big muscles.

"Give us the scroll and we won't hurt you!" the muscular man said, plucking the key from her hand.

"My grandpa has it!" she blurted out. "He took it to the police."

The skinny man looked at his partner, shook his head, and grumbled, "This job was supposed to be easy."

The stocky man held up his gun and pointed it at Cordelia. She fainted, hitting her head hard on the floor.

5

When Cordelia awakened, she found herself strapped in the back seat of an SUV. She kept her emotions in check and tried not to cry.

Where are we going? How long was I passed out? She frantically wondered.

The night sky whizzed past her window as they traveled along a deserted highway. Nothing looked familiar. The skinny man with tattoos was driving while the stocky man with muscles sat in the passenger seat. Trying not draw attention to herself, she closed her eyes and listened to their conversation.

"What's the plan?" the stocky man asked.

"Call Dad when we get to our cabin on the Mystique River," the skinny man responded.

She heard a foot nervously tapping on the floor board of the vehicle.

Dad? Cordelia thought. *Are these guys Viktor's kids?*

Cordelia opened her eyes as the SUV's headlights shined upon a creepy old cabin. The paint on the wood siding and shutters was chipped and worn. The bushes and lawn were overgrown. It looked as though it had been vacant for some time.

The SUV rolled to a stop, and the two men jumped out. The

stocky man unbuckled Cordelia's seat belt and threw her over his shoulder. He carried her into the cabin, kicked the door open to one of the bedrooms, and threw her onto the bed. Musty old dust flew up and made her cough.

"Stay there and don't move," the burly man commanded. "And don't make a sound."

His callous words frightened her to the core. She lay frozen on the bed watching his every move. She clenched her fists ready to defend herself.

The other thug came into the room with a hammer and a few planks of wood. He nailed the boards to the wall, blocking any access to the window. After he finished, the two men left the bedroom and locked the door behind them. Cordelia tried prying off the boards, but they wouldn't budge. She paced the room, planning her escape.

The men began talking in the living room. She pressed her ear to the door and listened.

"Hello, Dad? Yeah, it's Rio. Murphy and I are hiding out at the cabin."

Recognizing the voice, Cordelia realized the skinny man's name was Rio.

"Yes. We have the girl and the skeleton key," Rio said.

After a long pause, Rio said with frustration, "What were we supposed to do? She didn't have the scroll."

Someone paced the floor and groaned.

"But she doesn't have it anymore," Rio stammered. "She said her grandpa has it."

Rio paused a moment and listened to Viktor's orders.

"Arrrgh, fine!" Rio shouted. He slammed the phone on the receiver.

"What did he say?" the other voice, Murphy, asked.

"He's glad we have the key, but he really wanted the scroll. He says we screwed up the job because we took the girl," Rio replied.

Murphy groaned again.

"The police took Dad down to the station to ask him questions," Rio continued. "The police searched Dad's property, but they didn't find any evidence. They haven't tied Dad to us... yet."

Murphy let out sigh of relief.

"Dad is coming up here in the morning," Rio added.

"What if the cops follow him?"

"He's a suspect, but they have no proof," Rio replied. "He said he would make sure no one was following him."

"So, what's the plan?" Murphy gruffly asked.

"Exchange the girl for the scroll. We'll take turns watching her. You sleep first, and then we'll switch later."

"Okay," Murphy responded.

Cordelia heard a door close and a TV turn on. She paced the floor for hours until her legs hurt and her mind frazzled. The room didn't have a clock, but she knew it was late. Crying until she had no tears, she collapsed onto the bed and fell asleep.

~

"Wake up!" Rio shouted.

Cordelia jolted awake, and she sprang to her feet. Her clothes were wrinkled, her hair was a mess, and her neck felt sore. Rio grabbed her by the wrist and pulled her into the living room.

Sunlight peeked through the curtains. Murphy sat on a dusty old couch while Viktor stood in front of him. Viktor turned his head and scowled at her.

Will my grandpa find me before it's too late? Cordelia feared. *Are they going to hurt me?*

"Sit down," Rio commanded.

Cordelia sat on the couch at the opposite end, away from Murphy. They scared her, but she knew as long as she remained alive Viktor had a chance of getting the scroll. Without Cordelia, Rio and Murphy had no chance of receiving their money.

"Where's the skeleton key?" Viktor asked.

Rio reached into his pocket, pulled out the key, and handed it to him.

"So, what's the plan?" Rio asked.

"In the middle of the night, I shoved a letter under the door of her grandpa's trailer," Viktor responded. "I told him to meet me at a specific location with the scroll and without the police. If he follows the rules, no one gets hurt."

"Can we trust him? What if the cops show up?" Rio asked.

"I'll stop them with this," Viktor replied while holding up the key.

"And what are you going to do with that? Throw it at them?" Rio chuckled, looking perplexed.

"Have you ever heard the story about Benjamin Franklin and the kite?" Viktor asked.

"I read about it when I was a kid. What does that have to do with us?" Rio asked skeptically.

"One stormy afternoon in Philadelphia, Benjamin Franklin and his son went outside to test the electrical nature of lightning. He took a key and attached it to a kite and flew it in the sky," Viktor said. "But only I discovered how to harness the electrical power of a thunderstorm with my key."

Murphy crossed his arms.

"I've used it once, a long time ago. I raised the key in the air and a lightning bolt blew a hole in the side of a ferry that I was standing on. I never used the key again, but now I may have no choice."

Rio looked at the key and shook his head in disbelief.

"Dad, you never told us this story. Are you losing your mind?" Murphy asked.

"I'm not crazy! It's the truth," Viktor said, pointing the key toward the sky.

Thunder rumbled outside and shook the cabin. Looking out the window, Cordelia saw clouds cover the morning sun.

"Why do you want the scroll?" Rio asked.

Before Viktor could answer, someone banged on the front door.

"It's the police! Run!" Murphy shouted as he sprang from the couch.

Murphy picked Cordelia up by her waist, threw her over his shoulder, and took off toward the back door. A split second later, the police kicked in the front door. Their guns were drawn.

6

Raindrops soaked Cordelia's clothes as Murphy ran down a sharp incline toward the Mystique River. A wooden boardwalk snaked along the riverbank, and sailboats floated toward Lake Michigan. When he reached the bottom of the hill, Murphy threw her over the guardrail onto the boardwalk. Her feet stung and her teeth chattered as she landed on the wood planks with a thud. Hunched over in pain, she slowly stood as Murphy climbed over the rail. She tried to run away, but he grabbed her arm and held it in a vice-like grip.

"Not so fast! You're my hostage," Murphy grunted.

She shivered at his callous words.

Is he going to kill me?

Viktor and Rio ran down the hill with the police right behind them. Viktor stopped, turned around, and raised the key above his head. When the policemen were a few yards away, Viktor pointed the key at the ground, just below their feet. The tip of the key glowed red and released a blinding flash of light. Cordelia covered her eyes as the lightning bolt scorched the earth. The shockwave knocked the officers to the ground like bowling pins.

Rio helped Viktor over the guardrail before he climbed over.

"Where are we going?" Murphy asked, slightly out of breath.

Viktor pointed east and said, "There's a marina on the other side of the bridge. I have a boat waiting there for us."

Murphy dragged Cordelia by her elbow along the boardwalk toward the Mystique Bridge. He was cutting off the circulation in her arm, leaving her hand feeling numb. Struggling to keep pace with him, she tripped on a loose plank and fell to her knees.

Frustrated, Murphy picked her up by her waist and threw her over his shoulder again. He wrapped one arm around her thighs and squeezed them.

Unable to move her legs, she beat her fists against his back.

"Let me go!" Cordelia shouted.

"Quiet!" Murphy grunted. "Or I'll snap your legs like twigs!"

She stopped resisting and looked back toward the cabin. The police regrouped and chased after them with their guns drawn.

Struggling to keep pace with the younger men, Viktor trailed a few yards behind, panting and cursing.

Startled pedestrians jumped out of the way as the gang ran along the boardwalk. They climbed the stairs leading up to the Mystique drawbridge.

When they reached the center of the bridge, a police car raced down Main Street. Sliding sideways, the car came to a screeching halt in front of them. Murphy stopped dead in his tracks and set Cordelia down on the sidewalk. Police cars blocked the north and south ends of the road, trapping them in the middle. Blue and red lights flashed as the sirens fell silent and the officers took cover behind their vehicles.

"What do we do now?" Rio asked.

Viktor put Cordelia on her feet, but he grabbed her around the throat with one arm and said, "We're not going down without a fight."

"Let's handle this peacefully," an officer announced through a bull horn. "Let the girl go."

"You can have the girl. All I want is the scroll," Viktor shouted.

Viktor has the key, why does he want more power? Cordelia asked herself, struggling beneath Viktor's arm.

He held up the skeleton key with his free hand and pointed it at the police. Feeling threatened, the officers raised their weapons and aimed.

Cordelia's mind raced. She knew if Viktor shot a lightning bolt at the police, they would be destroyed. Finding her chance to escape, she bit Viktor's arm and kicked him in the shin with her heel. His free arm erratically swung in the air as the tip of the key glowed red.

BANG!

A bright flash of lightning shot from the key and struck the ground in front of Cordelia. Murphy and Rio dove for cover.

The shockwave slammed against Cordelia's chest. Her head snapped backward and struck Viktor in the jaw. He released his grip on her and stumbled backward. His back hit the guardrail and the key flew out of his hand. With her ears still ringing, Cordelia peered over the guardrail and watched the key splash into the river.

Without thinking, she climbed onto the top of the railing and dove off the bridge. She kept her toes pointed in the air with her back arched. The dive would've been a perfect 10, if it were being scored at a competition. Abandoning all her fear, she plunged into the abyss.

7

The water felt cold on Cordelia's skin as she swam to the murky bottom. Without a shred of light, she used her sense of touch to guide her. Slimy seaweed and scaly fish brushed against her legs. She dragged her fingertips along the muddy river bed, and with pressure building up in her lungs, she wondered, *How much longer can I hold my breath?*

Her hand brushed against a metal object. She clenched the key in her fist and swam upward.

Popping her head above the water's surface, her heart filled with joy when she saw Grandpa Albert pacing back and forth on the boardwalk. She swam to the riverbank. His face lit up when he saw her. He leaned over, stretched out his hand, and pulled her to shore.

Giving her a bear hug, he whispered, "I was scared I lost you."

Although dripping wet, she felt warm and secure in his arms. After their embrace, he held her hand while they walked along the boardwalk toward the bridge. They climbed up the stairs, and when they reached the top, Cordelia saw the police officers putting handcuffs on Rio and Murphy. They led Viktor to a police car and put him inside.

An officer approached Cordelia and Albert.

"I'm Detective Loch," he stated, handing Cordelia a towel. "Are you okay?"

Cordelia nodded.

"That was pretty brave of you to jump off the bridge," the

detective said.

"And dangerous," Albert added.

"I already have your grandfather's statement, but I'll need your side of the story, too," the detective explained.

She wrapped herself in the towel and shivered as she relayed her experience.

"Thank for your detailed description," the detective stated. "Did you find the key?"

"Yes," she replied.

"Can I have it? I need it for evidence."

"Yes," Albert agreed, looking at Cordelia. "It's safer with the police."

Cordelia reluctantly handed the detective the key, even though she wanted to keep it.

"But whatever you do, don't let Viktor near it," Albert warned. "He'll use it again."

"Maybe it was a fluke storm," the detective said, shrugging his shoulders. "In any case, we'll test it out to make sure it's not a weapon."

"But Viktor is the only one who can use it that way," Albert pleaded.

"Don't worry. We have everything under control; you're free to go," Detective Loch said. "We'll call you if we have any more questions on the investigation. We can handle the rest. Thank you."

Albert reluctantly nodded.

As the detective walked way, Albert whispered to Cordelia, "I warned him. It's out of our hands now. Let's go home."

～

As Albert drove back to Whitehall, Cordelia struggled to make sense of what had happened.

"Grandpa," she said with a question lingering in the back of her mind.

"Yes, sweetie?"

"How did you find me?"

"When I realized you were missing, I panicked and called the police." Albert began his story, and his voice became agitated. "I waited for hours while they did their investigation. I tried to sleep, but I tossed and turned in bed. In the middle of the night, I went outside for some fresh air, and I found a letter. It said I had to bring the scroll to a field up north, and if I brought the police they would hurt you."

Intrigued by the story, she nodded.

"I couldn't wait for the police to fix the problem," Albert said, puffing out his chest. "I was determined to find you. In that moment, I remembered Viktor's story about the scroll."

"Yes, now we know it works," Cordelia added.

"I thought, *What if I could become a real fortune teller?*" Albert said with glimmer in his eye. "I could use the crystal ball to find you. I figured I had nothing to lose so I sat down at the table in my camper, and I read the spell out loud. It worked!"

"Wow!" Cordelia exclaimed, finally believing in the power of the Secret Talent Scroll.

"Using the crystal ball, I found your location," he added. "I told the police and we tracked you down."

"Thanks for saving me," she whispered.

"You're welcome."

"You never told me the story of how you got the crystal ball," she said.

"When we get home, I'll show you."

"Really? How?" Cordelia asked, raising her eyebrows.

"I'll show you the past with the crystal ball," Albert said with a smile.

8

⁓

The lights were turned low, and crickets chirped outside. Albert grabbed the crystal ball from a book shelf, set it on the kitchen table, and sat down next to Cordelia.

"Are you ready to see the past?" Albert asked with a twinkle in his eye.

She nodded, waiting for the crystal ball to work its magic.

Albert waved his hands over the ball, and purple smoke swirled around inside the glass. The smoke parted, revealing an image of a young man with wavy tan hair playing a piano in a crowded dance hall. Like an old family movie on a projection screen, the crystal ball played images from the past.

"Who's that?" Cordelia asked.

"That's me," Albert said, leaning back and rubbing his forehead. "I was so young... maybe nineteen or twenty years old."

A woman with shiny dark hair and piercing green eyes stepped up to the microphone and sang in front of the dancing teenagers.

"Is that Grandma Elsa?" Cordelia asked.

"Yes," Albert said wistfully as his face lit up. "She had such a beautiful voice. We created music that made everyone want to dance."

Cordelia smiled.

The younger Albert finished the song and followed Elsa back to a table. A tall gentleman with a fancy suit and a woman with curly red hair sat at the table with Albert and Elsa.

"Those are your great-grandparents, Niles and Coral," Albert said, pointing at the crystal ball. "Elsa's parents owned a traveling circus. They were looking for someone who could play music at their show, so they hosted a talent competition at a club in Chicago."

Young Albert made quick glances at Elsa as he talked to Niles. After sharing a laugh, he reached across the table and shook Niles' hand.

"That's the night I joined the circus," Albert said with pride. "I accepted the offer because I wanted to be closer to Elsa."

"You chased after Grandma?" Cordelia asked with a grin. She had never heard that story.

The crystal ball flickered as though it was changing movie reels. The images fast-forwarded to show Albert asking Elsa to marry him. After the wedding ceremony, the married couple unwrapped a gift box containing a crystal ball.

"Niles thought I would make a great fortune teller because I was always giving people advice," Albert explained. "During the day I was the fortune teller, and at night I played music for the show. Those were the happiest days of my life."

Albert's face glowed.

"Elsa and I took over the circus after her parents passed away," Albert explained. "But that was before you were born."

The crystal ball's images swirled, now showing an image of a gravestone with words: "Elsa Da Vinci, loving wife, mother, and friend." The tiny movie sped up, showing a much older Albert selling his piano. Purple smoke clouded over the image, and the crystal ball went dark.

Albert rested his elbows on the table and covered his face with his hands as his body trembled.

"Grandpa, are you okay?" Cordelia asked, placing her hand on his shoulder.

"I miss her so much," he said, tears cascading down his cheek.

Cordelia leaned over and gave him a hug.

"Me too," she said with a lump in her throat.

"Since your grandma passed away, I haven't had the heart to play music."

Cordelia wanted to take away his pain, but there was nothing she could do or say that would fix the hole in his heart. She stayed with him late into the evening until they grew tired and he went to bed. Feeling secure in his camper, she lay down on the couch. Tonight she didn't want to be alone.

~

Cordelia sat at the table in her parents' camper, writing in her journal. The door creaked open. Her face lit up when she saw her parents had come back from their vacation. Jumping from her seat, she ran to the door and wrapped her arms around them.

Gala kissed her on the forehead and said, "We missed you."

"Me too," Cordelia said. "I have to tell you something! The scroll has magic powers and Grandpa used it to find me in Mystique. And…"

"What? Slow down," Salvatore interrupted her. "We just got home. Let us settle in first and then you can tell us your story."

"Okay," Cordelia replied, trying to remain calm.

After her parents unpacked, they came back into the kitchen and sat down at the table. Cordelia frantically told them the story about how she was kidnapped and how Albert used the Secret Talent Scroll and the crystal ball to find her.

"Wait, slow down, Cordelia, you were kidnapped!?" Salvatore asked with anger in his voice. "Why didn't anyone call us?"

"It happened so fast," Cordelia replied.

"Are you okay?" Gala asked with concern.

"Yeah… I'm okay, don't worry," Cordelia stammered, realizing that rushing into the story wasn't the best way to tell her parents about the events from the last few days.

"Thankfully, you weren't hurt," Salvatore responded. He looked distraught, and his hands shook.

"I'm sorry. I shouldn't have blurted it out like that," Cordelia added.

"Are you sure you're okay, honey?" Gala asked, her eyes narrowing a bit as she pulled Cordelia into a hug.

"I'm fine." Cordelia's words were muffled as her face pressing into her mother's shoulder.

Salvatore sighed. "I'm glad you're safe, but we need to talk about security."

"I agree with your father," Gala said.

"Viktor is in jail now," Cordelia said. "But I'll have to testify at the trial."

"And this scroll..." Salvatore started. "Your grandfather has it?"

Cordelia nodded.

"Okay, well let's make sure it stays with him," he said. "I'll have a talk with him about it."

Salvatore wrapped his arms around Cordelia.

~

September 7th
Delta Training and Swim Center, Grand Rapids, MI

The first week of school had been a whirlwind of activities preparing for the Olympic tryouts. Between homework and swim practice, Cordelia nearly forgot about the scroll. But the big day finally arrived and there she stood on top of the diving platform, waiting for her cue to perform.

Her mind filled with images of the future. She pictured a gold medal, being on commercials, and leaving the circus behind. With her heart pounding, Cordelia let out a long breath of air. She took three steps and stumbled. She regained her balance and leaped off the diving board. Her head wobbled and her shoulders were slumped throughout the dive.

SPLASH!

9

~

*F*inal score six out of ten, I failed! Cordelia cursed. *I'll never be on the Olympic Swim Team. Now what am I going to do?*

She replayed all of her little mistakes over and over again. She didn't straighten her arms at the right moment. She didn't focus on her balance and form. Instead her mind was preoccupied with Olympic dreams. Dreams make life exciting, but hers vanished with a big splash.

Am I living in a nightmare? she wondered with frayed nerves.

She stormed into the empty locker room, ripped off her swimming cap, and threw it to the floor. Her red hair slapped against her face. She hung her head as she sat on the cold metal bench in front of her locker. Tears streamed down her cheeks as water dripped off the bathing suit her mother had made for her, forming a puddle beneath her feet.

She hadn't achieved the thrill of victory. Instead, the agony of defeat stabbed her in the heart. Through the concrete block walls she heard the crowd cheer for the winners, which made the pain sting even more. All of her hard work and sacrifices seemed pointless.

Should I try again in another four years?

A sharp knock on the locker room door jarred her attention. *I hope that's my parents, so I can go home,* she thought bitterly. She wanted to disappear.

"Cordelia, are you in there?" her coach called out.

She didn't want to see the disappointment in his eyes. She reluctantly stood up, walked over to the door, and opened it a crack. Coach John stood outside the locker room. He had beach-blonde hair and a stubbly beard. He wore a red tank top shirt that showed off his biceps.

"I know you're feeling down, but I have some good news for you," John said with a smile.

Cordelia scoffed. "Nothing could make me happy right now."

"Ariel dropped out of the hundred-meter freestyle event and you're her replacement!"

"Wait, what did you just say?" Cordelia asked. Her heart rate doubled in a split second.

"Sorry I didn't tell you. I didn't want you to be distracted during your diving competition."

"But I'm not ready," she countered, feeling the gravity of the situation sink in.

"You're ready. We practiced all the techniques. Trust your gut on this one."

She shook her head in disbelief.

"You can do this," Coach John said with confidence.

"Give me a minute," she replied, letting the door close behind her.

In a daze, she walked back to the bench and plopped down.

Can I face another disappointment?

Looking down at her gym bag, she remembered bringing the Secret Talent Scroll. She wanted to win the competition on her own merit, but she had brought the scroll just in case. It was still a mystery to her. She didn't know how it worked, but it might be her last option for winning the race.

My swimsuit could represent my talent and I could use the scroll to become the fastest swimmer in the world, she dreamed. *This might be my only way out of the circus.*

She opened the bag and reached inside for the parchment.

Am I cheating? She wrestled with her emotions.

She knew the scroll was dangerous, but she didn't have time to think about the ramifications of her actions. It was now or never. Her hesitation was overcome by her ambition to succeed.

She unrolled the scroll and whispered the words on the page, "I call upon the four classical elements: wind, fire, earth and water. Wind moves sand. Fire creates earth and ash. Earth absorbs water. Water quenches fire. With my swimsuit, give me the power to be the fastest swimmer in the world."

A strong wind from underneath the locker room door kicked up sand and swirled around in a tiny dust tornado. The sand grains collided, creating tiny sparks. She felt the heat as the cloud spun around her body.

Baffled and intrigued, she sat frozen on the bench.

The sparks ignited into tiny fireballs. She crouched to avoid the flames. The sink faucet turned and a long spout of water flew across the room and extinguished the fire. The sand particles turned into blackened ash, fluttered down onto her green bathing suit where they dissolved into the fabric.

She felt lightheaded, and a tingling sensation ran through her body. Her leg, arms, and core muscles felt stronger and alert for action. As though she had a photographic memory, all the swim maneuvers and techniques from her coach flooded into her mind.

An invisible force in the room turned off the sink faucets, and the gust of wind subsided. All went silent.

A knock on the locker room door broke her trance. She stood up and sprinted to the door.

Her coach paced back and forth.

"Hurry up, you're next," he commanded. "If you miss this opportunity, you'll be disqualified."

Cordelia grabbed her swim cap and raced behind her coach to the pool. The bleachers were filled with parents, family members, and athletes. Her body filled with adrenaline, and her heart pulsated with energy. Her Olympic dream was still alive.

10

~

Adjusting her swim goggles, Cordelia stood on the diving block waiting for the starter signal to go off. This time she was completely focused.

BEEP!

In perfect form, she dove into the pool with her hands above her head in a streamlined position. Slightly bending her knees, she used her hips and thighs to cut through the water like a dolphin. Rotating her body to the surface, she inhaled through her mouth. In a matter of seconds she reached the end of the 50-meter pool. She flipped her body by doing a somersault underwater and used both her legs to propel herself off the pool wall for the final lap.

The seconds flew by in a blur. When her fingertips touched the opposite end of the pool, she popped her head above the water and took a deep breath. The audience cheered as she pushed her goggles up onto her forehead. Glancing at the time clock, she burst into tears; her time nearly beat the women's world record for the event. She climbed out of the pool and raised her fist up in victory.

Ariel, one of her swim teammates, limped over on crutches. She had compression tape wrapped around her right foot.

"Congratulations," Ariel said halfheartedly. "Coach said we should support each other."

Ariel must be mad because I took her place and won the competition.

"Thank you," she replied. "What happened to your foot?"

"I sprained my ankle," Ariel said, gritting her teeth.

"That's terrible," Cordelia replied with a tinge of guilt. She was Ariel's replacement after all, but Cordelia couldn't change that.

"Nice bathing suit," Ariel snickered. "Did your mom make it for you?"

Cordelia's face turned red, and she gave Ariel an evil stare. It was true; she didn't have any fancy designer clothes. Everything she wore was handmade, but she tried not to be envious of everyone else.

Without replying, she watched Ariel hobble back toward the bleachers.

Coach John sprinted over to the edge of the pool with a towel.

"Ariel is just upset. Don't let her bother you," Coach John said with a frown. "I'll have a word with her afterwards. She shouldn't talk to you like that."

Cordelia lifted her chin and nodded with a glimmer in her eye as she dried off with the towel.

"Great job!" Coach John exclaimed, giving her a high five.

"Thanks!"

She giggled when he did a little victory dance.

Her parents jumped from their seats and approached them.

"You did a great job, sweetie," Gala said, giving her a hug.

"Very impressive," Salvatore added, brushing back Cordelia's hair.

"Thanks, Dad."

A sharply dressed woman from the audience walked over and introduced herself. She turned to Cordelia and said, "Congratulations! Your performance was excellent."

"Thanks," Cordelia replied.

"I represent a sporting goods manufacturer," the woman said. "We're launching a new swimsuit line and we wondered if you would consider endorsing our product. The Olympics could be the beginning of something exciting for you and your future. Here's my card." The woman handed a business card to Salvatore. "Give me a call, and we'll iron out the details when you make it to the Olympics."

"Okay!" Cordelia said. Her dreams were starting to come true.

The woman's high heels clicked on the poolside tile as she walked away.

"Well, we have a lot to discuss when we get home," Salvatore said with pride. "We'll meet you in the lobby after you change. Don't take too long, okay, sweetie?"

"Okay, Dad, I'll be there soon."

As Cordelia walked toward the locker room, she ran into Marcel. Marcel was one of the school's best weight lifters. He was also training for the Olympics in the power lifting category, and Coach John was his coach, too. Marcel had a solid frame with huge muscles for his age, and his brown eyes matched his dark hair.

"Hey!" he exclaimed. "I was looking for you."

"Hey, Marcel... You were?" she asked, blushing.

"Yeah, I wanted tell you congratulations on the win!" he said with a confident smile. He stared into her eyes, making her feel giddy.

"Thank you," she said as a smile spread across her face.

Her mind drifted into a memory from their writing class in school. Marcel sat in the front row while Cordelia sat in back. He and his friend, Kyle, were talking about the girls-ask-guys dance. They were naming all of the pretty girls and commenting on which girls they hoped would ask them to the dance.

She had wanted to ask Marcel for a few weeks, but was too shy to approach him. She never had a chance to talk to him alone; he was always surrounded by his friends at lunch or in the hall. She wasn't even sure if he knew her name. Finally, she had built up the courage to ask him.

As she walked over to talk to him, she overheard Marcel say to Kyle, "I don't want any weird girls asking me to the dance."

Cordelia's heart sank; she always felt like an awkward circus girl. Embarrassed, she never asked Marcel or anyone else to the dance.

"You almost set a new record! How did you pull that off?" Marcel asked.

She snapped back to the present moment.

"To be honest, I had some luck," she said, lifting her eyes to meet his.

"Could you send it my way?" he chuckled as he turned and walked away.

Feeling disappointed by his departure, she wanted him to stay and pay more attention to her because she liked it.

"Maybe I can help you win, too!" she blurted out. If she helped him, he would never ignore her again.

Marcel stopped and slowly turned around.

"Really? How?" he asked, raising his eyebrows.

"Follow me," she replied, feeling a burst of self-confidence as a result of her recent victory.

11

~

Cordelia ran into the locker room, changed into her dry clothes, and grabbed the scroll from her duffle bag.

"What are you going to do with that?" Marcel asked, scratching his head.

"You'll see," she responded.

With Marcel by her side, they searched the sports complex looking for a private place to talk. Down one of the corridors, they found a gym where athletes could warm up with free weights. She looked around to make sure it was empty.

"So what's your plan?" he asked.

She held up the scroll and said, "This has a magic spell that turns your talents into extraordinary powers."

"Sounds like hocus pocus to me," he said with a chuckle.

"I won the competition after using it."

"Really?" he asked with skepticism.

"And I think it can help you win your competition, too."

"Sure, why not?" he asked, shrugging his shoulders. "I have nothing to lose. How does it work?"

"You're going to need that," she said, pointing at two 50-pound dumbbells.

He picked up the weights and held them in his hands.

She unrolled the scroll and began the chant, "I call upon the four classical elements: wind, fire, earth, and water. Wind moves sand. Fire creates earth and ash. Earth absorbs water. Water quenches fire.

Give Marcel more muscular power with his dumbbells."

A gust of wind blew open the gym door.

"What is going on?" he muttered.

The wind swirled around the room creating a small tornado of sand. As the particles collided, a tiny fireworks show danced before their eyes. From a water fountain on the far side of the gym, a spout shot across the room and extinguished the flames. The sand turned to ash. The soot fell on Marcel's dumbbells. The wind subsided and the water fountain shut off. His eyes glazed over as if he were in a trance.

"Are you okay?" she asked, snapping her fingers.

"Yeah," he replied, wavering for a moment. "I feel a little dizzy."

As he lifted the weights, his muscles bulged from his arms all the way down to his toes. Within minutes, he grew four inches taller.

"Stop!" she yelled. "You're getting too big. Don't forget they weighed you in before the competition."

Emboldened by his newfound strength, he looked in the mirror on the gym wall and admired his muscles.

"Wow! This is so cool!" he said as a smile spread across his face, appearing drunk in the moment.

He leaned down and gave her a hug. As she smelled his cologne, her heart began to flutter.

"Thank you so much!" he said.

"You're welcome," she stammered.

"Can you stay and watch my competition?" he asked.

She grinned and nodded.

"Cool," he said and sprinted out the door.

She chased after him, barely keeping up.

⁓

Cordelia wanted to see Marcel win his competition, but first, she had to get her parents to agree to stay.

"Mom! Dad!" Cordelia called to them as she ran down the hall and into the main lobby of the training center. Cordelia rushed past some people who were leaving the auditorium. Her parents stood next to a showcase with photographs and trophies won by previous athletes. Salvatore held up his car keys and waved.

"What is it, hon?" Gala asked, sliding the strap of her purse over her shoulder.

"My friend, Marcel, is competing for a spot in the Olympics too," Cordelia said. "He's a power lifter. He's almost up—can we stay and watch him?"

Her parents looked at each other.

"Who's this young man?" Salvatore asked with concern. "You didn't tell us you had a boyfriend."

Cordelia blushed as her mom gently squeezed Cordelia's shoulder.

"Yes," Gala said, "Who is Marcel, and why don't we know about him?"

"He's not my boyfriend. He's a boy I like from school," Cordelia explained. "We share a few classes together. Can we please stay and watch his competition?"

Salvatore pulled out the pocket watch and rubbed his forehead. "I'm not sure if we have enough time. I'm kinda getting hungry."

Gala paused for a moment before replying, "Sure, sweetie. We can stay for a few minutes."

"Thanks, Mom!" Cordelia beamed with excitement.

"Okay," Salvatore reluctantly agreed. "But I'll need to meet him and his parents at some point."

Cordelia nodded. Her parents followed her into the auditorium where the power lifters were competing, and they sat down in the bleachers.

The announcer spoke over the loud speaker, "Our final competitor in the one-hundred five kilogram weightlifting event is Marcel Duchamp. If Marcel is successful, he'll move to the next phase of the Olympic trials."

Marcel stepped up to the chalk box and applied chalk to his sweaty palms. Looking nervous, he stood in front of the barbell with his feet shoulder-width apart. He squatted, picked up the barbell, and rested it on his shoulders. Kicking one foot back, he pointed his elbows forward and raised the barbell over his head.

Cordelia threw her fist in the air and shouted, "He did it!"

The audience stood up and cheered.

Marcel dropped the barbell. It landed with a thud and bounced. He walked off the floor mat. Coach John ran over to Marcel, patted him the back, and gave him a high-five.

One of the judges stood up and walked over to Coach John. After talking for a few moments, John's face turned bright red. He threw his hands up in the air and shook his head. The audience fell silent.

What's going on? Cordelia wondered.

The judge walked back to his table with the other judges and sat down.

A voice crackled over the speakers and announced, "Marcel Duchamp's performance is under review."

After a few minutes the announcer said, "Marcel is disqualified until further notice."

The crowd in the bleachers murmured. Marcel stormed toward the exit and kicked the door open with his foot, leaving the crumpled door barely hanging on one hinge.

Cordelia was crushed.

What have I done? Was it my fault Marcel was disqualified? He'll never speak to me again!

She wanted to run after Marcel, apologize, and beg for his forgiveness.

"Cordelia, honey," Gala said, placing her hand on Cordelia's shoulder. "Are you okay?"

Cordelia's eyes were frozen on the mangled door.

"Honey?" Salvatore asked. "Are you okay?"

Cordelia snapped out of it. "Yeah... Sorry... I feel bad for Marcel..."

"I understand, sweetie," Gala said gently. "But... Maybe he took something he wasn't supposed to."

"No! He wouldn't do that!"

"All right, all right," Salvatore said. "Your mother was just being realistic. We feel bad for him too," Salvatore rubbed Cordelia's upper back, trying to soothe her. "Let's head home. We'll stop at your favorite restaurant and celebrate."

"Um..." Cordelia mumbled. "Okay, we can go home."

~

Cordelia remained silent as they drove to the restaurant, but her parents couldn't contain their excitement.

"We're so proud of you," Salvatore gushed. "You've worked so hard, and it paid off! We're so happy for you."

"You did an amazing job, honey," Gala added.

"Thanks."

"Aren't you proud of yourself?" Salvatore asked. "You should be."

"Yeah... I am," Cordelia responded. "I'm still thinking about Marcel, sorry."

"Well, we know you feel bad, but it's time to celebrate. This is a big deal!" Salvatore exclaimed, looking at her in the rearview mirror.

The car started to shimmy, and the tires groaned.

"What's that noise?" Gala asked.

"I think it's the tires," Salvatore grumbled. "Arrgh! Guess what we're spending our next paycheck on."

Gala stared out the window, biting her lip.

"Cordelia, while you were in the locker room getting dressed, I called your grandfather and told him the good news," Salvatore changed the subject. "He's meeting us for dinner."

She wished her grandpa had been at the competition, but he had a lot to pack up before the circus headed south.

"Good, they don't look busy," Salvatore said as he pulled into the restaurant parking lot.

They were seated at a table for four, and within minutes, Albert arrived to join them.

"Congratulations, kiddo!" Albert exclaimed.

"Thanks, Grandpa," she said.

"Wow, the Olympics! A sponsorship!? What a night!" he said, giving her a hug. "I am so proud of you."

"Thank you, Grandpa," Cordelia responded. "I'm excited, too!"

"Rightly so," Albert said, letting her go.

Everyone opened their menus and made small talk about what sounded good.

When the waitress approached, she asked, "How's everyone doing tonight?"

Salvatore didn't give anyone else a chance to respond. "Fantastic! Our daughter just qualified at her swim meet for the Olympics!" He beamed at Cordelia.

"Wow, that's amazing!" the waitress said, looking impressed.

"Dad...." Cordelia blushed.

"We're just proud, honey," Gala said, placing a hand on her daughter's shoulder.

"What can I get everyone?" the waitress asked.

The rest of dinner was filled with what-if talk: What if Cordelia made it to the Olympics? What if she was sponsored by that swimsuit company? What if she won a gold medal?!

It was all a bit much to hear and handle, but Cordelia relished her parents' love and support. She knew that no matter what, she could accomplish anything as long as she had her family by her side.

12

~

In the morning, Gala drove Cordelia to Siren Bay High School.

"Don't forget that after your swim practice, we're having dinner with your dad and grandpa before they pack up the circus and head out of town," Gala reminded her as she dropped her off at school.

Cordelia and her mom stayed behind at the family cabin in Siren Bay while she attended school. She wouldn't see her father or grandfather again until Christmas and then again on her spring break. But during the summer, she traveled with them all over Michigan, hitting every major festival.

As Cordelia walked down the school hallway, she saw Marcel standing in front of his locker with his forehead pressed against the door. She felt heartbroken for him and also responsible for his disqualification.

"I'm so sorry," she said as she approached him. She placed her hand on his shoulder.

He punched the locker with his fist, causing a dent. Frightened, Cordelia withdrew her hand from his shoulder and stepped backward. He spun around and gave her an angry stare.

"My life is ruined!" he stammered. His red eyes fought back tears. "And all you have to say is 'sorry.' I'm barred from any Olympic competitions! When they did a blood test they found abnormal levels of hormones in my system."

"I didn't know this would happen!" Cordelia cried.

"This is your fault!"

He turned around and stormed down the hall with his books. The reason she had helped him was because she wanted to get to know him better.

She turned around when she heard Coach John's voice say, "Cordelia, I can't believe what happened to Marcel."

Coach John stood across the hall in front of his classroom door. Not only was he a coach, but he also taught Algebra. He crossed his arms and shook his head in disbelief.

"What happened after I left the tryouts?" Cordelia asked.

"The judges reweighed Marcel and tested him for steroids. They think he cheated," Coach John explained. "They didn't find anything illegal, but they agreed something wasn't right. He does look taller and his muscles are bigger than I remember. But how could his muscles grow so fast?"

"I don't know," Cordelia replied.

She knew the scroll had something to do with it, but she kept her mouth shut. Besides, Coach John would never believe her. Even if he did, it wouldn't change the fact that Marcel would never compete again.

"After you left, Marcel tore apart the locker room," Coach John added.

"He did?" Cordelia said in shock.

"Yes," Coach John replied. "I tried to stop him, but his strength scared me. Now the owners of the auditorium want Marcel to pay for the damages."

"Are his parents paying for it?" she asked.

"I don't think so. He'll need to get a summer job."

The first warning bell rang.

Coach John tapped his watch and said, "Don't be late for class. And don't forget we have swim practice at the YMCA after school."

She nodded and hurried to her locker to collect her books.

~

After the final bell rang, Cordelia gathered her belongings from her locker and headed toward the school parking lot. Ariel stood next to her brand new BMW, a birthday present from her wealthy parents. Cordelia tried not be envious, but jealousy overcame her thoughts.

I'll never afford my own car! Sure, grandpa pays me to help my mom make clothes for the circus performers, but that's not enough... But if I get that endorsement deal, I can buy whatever car I want! I have to win a medal.

The loud muffler backfired as her mom pulled into the parking space next to Ariel's car. Cordelia blushed. Without saying a word to Ariel, Cordelia hopped into her parents' car. The door creaked and groaned when she closed the door.

"How was school?" her mom asked, pulling out of the parking lot and heading to the YMCA for swim practice.

Cordelia bit her bottom lip. All day her thoughts had been on Marcel and how she could fix things, but she didn't know how to express her feelings to her mother.

After a few minutes of silence, Gala raised her eyebrows and asked, "Is everything okay?"

Before Cordelia could respond, her mom's eyes opened wide. Her mother's pink cheeks turned white and her smile quickly faded as she opened her mouth in a scream.

BANG!

The sound of crunching metal and squealing tires stung her ears. Everything happened in slow motion. The passenger window shattered, scattering shards of glass all over the seat and dashboard; the glass particles cut Cordelia's cheeks and arms. The passenger door buckled, thrusting Cordelia over onto the center console. Lying on her ribcage, she felt the car spin around 360 degrees before crashing into a concrete curb. Her vision faded into black.

13

~

Cordelia's eyes fluttered open, and she struggled to focus. She found herself lying in a hospital bed with her dad and grandpa sitting next to her, intently watching her every move.

"She's awake, I'll get the doctor," Salvatore said, jumping up from his chair.

Albert reached out and squeezed Cordelia's hand.

A few minutes later, Salvatore returned with a short, bald doctor.

The doctor leaned over the bed rail and spoke in a monotone voice, "You were in an accident, Cordelia. You have knee fractures from where your legs hit the car dashboard. The tendons around your knees were torn, so we had to do surgery to stabilize the kneecaps."

Shaking her head in denial, she looked down and saw her legs wrapped in two white casts. They were elevated by a pulley system, and her toes were numb.

"For the next few days, you can't put a lot pressure on your legs. Once the casts come off, you'll need leg braces and crutches. With six to eight weeks of physical therapy, you should be able to walk again," the doctor said with some hesitation in his voice.

The news crashed down on Cordelia like a tidal wave, and she felt like she was swept away by an undertow.

As the doctor left the room, he said in low voice, "I'll be back tomorrow to check on you."

Feeling nauseous, she rubbed her forehead to ease her headache as the room began to spin.

"Where's Mom?" she asked.

"Your mom...oh my gosh, Gala...." Salvatore said with teary eyes and quivering lips. Her father covered his face with his hands and stepped into the hallway.

"Your mom..." Grandpa Albert choked up. "She died in the car crash."

Devastated, Cordelia grabbed her pillow, placed it over her face, and screamed. She rocked back and forth in bed. Feeling a warm hand touch her shoulder, she looked up and saw her grandpa sitting on the bed. Her legs began to throb and she winced in pain.

"Do you need more medication?" Albert asked with concern in his voice.

She nodded.

Albert pressed a button next to the bed. A few moments later, a nurse came into the room.

"Is everything okay?" the nurse asked.

Cordelia described her pain and anxiety.

"Okay, I'll be right back," the nurse reassured them.

The nurse left the room and after a few moments she returned with a small clear cup containing two white pills in one hand and a Styrofoam cup filled with water in the other.

"This should help," the nurse said, setting the pills and water on the nightstand. "It will calm your nerves."

With a shaky hand, Cordelia picked up the pills, tossed them into her mouth, and swallowed them. She took a sip of water as the nurse turned a dial on the wall and the overhead lights dimmed.

"You should get some rest so your body can heal faster," the nurse said before leaving the room again.

"It's okay, sweetheart," Albert said in a hushed tone. "I'll be right here."

The strong medication kicked in, and she drifted in and out of sleep.

~

The hospital door burst open with a loud thud. Cordelia propped herself up with her elbows. Her father stood at the foot of the bed with the Secret Talent Scroll in his hand.

"I can fix Cordelia's legs and bring back my wife!" Salvatore declared with a determined look on his face.

"How?" Albert asked, rubbing his forehead.

"I'm going to use the scroll to give me the power to go back in time and change the past with this!" Salvatore said, holding up the pocket watch.

Albert wrung his hands, paced the floor, and spoke with grave concern, "All the moments in life have a purpose, even in tragedy."

"But my pain is too great," Salvatore stammered.

"I can understand your grief, but I don't think we should do this," Albert cautioned. "What about the ramifications of having these powers?"

"It's worth the risk," Salvatore said, raising his voice. "It has to work!"

Can my dad fix things? Cordelia's mind filled with hope.

14

~

Salvatore held the pocket watch in the palm of his hands while Albert read the spell, "I call on the four classical elements, wind, fire, earth, and water. Wind moves sand. Fire creates earth and ash. Earth absorbs water. Water quenches fire. Give Salvatore the ability to control time and space with his pocket watch."

Cordelia's eyes widened when the hospital bed shook. The rising winds broke loose the window's latch, and the window flew open. A tornado of sand swirled around the pocket watch.

A flash lit up the night sky and was followed by a thunderous boom. A light bulb overhead shattered, sending sparks flying everywhere. The sparks ignited the sand in the cloud, causing it to burst into a tiny fireworks show. Defying gravity, small droplets of water rose up from the Styrofoam cup on the nightstand and extinguished the flames. The ashes sprinkled over the pocket watch and Salvatore's palm, dissolving into his skin.

The hands on the clock moved in opposite directions at high speeds. The pocket watch slowed down and kept pace with the current time as the wind subsided.

"Wow," Cordelia whispered. "That was crazy! What happened?"

Albert shrugged his shoulders.

"See if the watch can control time!" Cordelia spoke her thoughts aloud.

Her father nodded and stared at the watch.

The hospital door creaked opened, startling everyone.

The nurse popped her head into the room and asked, "Is everything okay in here?"

"Yes, we're okay," Albert replied.

"I heard breaking glass," the nurse said looking at the broken light bulbs on the floor; she walked over to the window and closed it. "It looks like a storm is moving in."

"Yes," Salvatore agreed. "It came on quite sudden."

"I'll get a broom and dustpan to clean up the glass," the nurse said. "How did the light break?"

"Maybe the lightning caused a power surge," Salvatore replied. "Do you have a moment?"

The nurse turned around and asked, "What is it?"

Salvatore raised the pocket watch to eye level and swung it like a pendulum on a grandfather clock.

Falling into a hypnotic state, the nurse's eyes glazed over and her body froze in time like a statue. Cordelia watched in awe as Salvatore controlled time right before her eyes!

As Salvatore swung the pocket watch, the nurse spoke really fast, "I'll be right back with the mop and broom."

She sped out of the room and quickly returned to clean up the mess. Her hands and arms moved in a blur as she swept the floor.

Salvatore stopped the watch and lowered his arm.

The nurse slowed down, and her movements returned to a normal speed.

"If it gets too hot in here, I can bring you a fan," the nurse said.

"Thank you," Salvatore replied as though nothing had transpired.

After the nurse left the room, Albert's face lit up and he said, "Wow, I can't believe you sped up time."

Salvatore's hands trembled and a bead of sweat dripped from his forehead. Staggering over to an empty chair, he sat down.

"Dad, are you okay?" Cordelia asked with concern.

"Yes, but I'm tired," he said, wiping his brow with his shirt cuff.

"What happened?" Albert asked.

"I felt a tingling sensation run through my fingers," Salvatore explained. "My mind was filled with all of Albert Einstein's theories and equations that I learned in college. Now that I know everything about physics, I have the ability to change time and space!"

Feeling dizzy, Cordelia rested her head on the pillow as she watched her father stand up and walk over to the bed. He raised the pocket watch to eye level and swung it back and forth. The watch melted into a blurry streak of gold, and she fell into a deep hypnotic state. Her eyelids closed.

15

~

Cordelia woke up in the hospital bed with casts on her legs. She clenched her teeth and screamed.

How long have I been asleep? she thought.

Salvatore paced the floor; his hair was disheveled, and he looked as though he hadn't slept in three days. Her grandpa sat in a chair next to the bed, wiping away his tears.

"Dad, what happened?" Cordelia asked. "Why am I still in bed? Why didn't you go back in time?"

He stopped pacing, looked in her eyes, and said, "I did go back in time. I went back a hundred times, but I couldn't fix the past."

His words crushed her heart.

"But...Why?" she stammered.

"I could see you, but you couldn't see me. I tried to warn you and your mom. The louder I spoke, the farther away you seemed. I could feel your presence, but I couldn't touch or interact with you. I couldn't pick up any objects. I was powerless to stop the accident. I was like a ghost, a faded memory of a person from the past."

"Did you save Mom?"

"No," Salvatore replied in a solemn voice.

Emotions crashed down upon her. They travelled in a full circle and came back to the same place where they started. She slammed her fists on the bed and cried.

"What do we do now?" Salvatore asked with frustration.

An idea popped into her head.

"What if we used the crystal ball to find a way to stop the accident?" she asked.

Albert's face lit up.

"I'll be back," he said as he bolted out of the room.

~

After an hour, Albert returned to the hospital and set the crystal ball on the nightstand.

"I hope this works," Albert said desperately.

Salvatore sat in the chair next to the bed with his elbows on the armrest. He clasped his hands together and raised them up to his chin. He stared into the core of the crystal ball and patiently waited for answers.

Albert waved his hands counter-clockwise. For the next hour, the crystal ball showed them everything Salvatore had tried with the pocket watch to stop the accident. None of the outcomes resulted in saving her mother's life or fixing Cordelia's legs. As though fate was set in stone, there had to be a purpose for her mother's death.

"There has to be a mathematical solution to this problem!" Salvatore shouted, gritting his teeth.

"Think back to your physics studies in college," Albert suggested. "Since you can use the pocket watch to manipulate time and space, is there something you can do to change the timing or move the objects?"

Salvatore closed his eyes in deep concentration as a bead of sweat developed on his brow, and his breathing accelerated.

After a few moments of mediation, Salvatore said, "In quantum mechanics, you could travel back in time to observe history, but there's no way of predicting or controlling the outcome. And the crystal ball hasn't provided any answers." He shook his fist in the air and said, "Why is this happening to me?"

"Maybe the scroll has limited power," Albert said with a trembling voice. "Or perhaps some things are meant to be. Maybe we need to accept the facts and go on from here."

"Dad, do you even care about me and my family?" Salvatore shouted. "Why aren't you helping me?"

"I'm not sure what else I can do," Albert replied as calmly as he could.

Salvatore stormed out of the room, slamming the door behind him.

Cordelia had lost her mom, and now her dad was slipping away. Her grandpa held her hand and squeezed it. His touch gave her some solace, but it couldn't take away her grief. Everything she loved died that day. Feeling empty inside, she cursed the day she found the scroll as her tears soaked the pillowcase.

16

~

A few days later…

For a brief minute, Cordelia hoped that the accident was a dream, that her mother was still alive, that she wasn't lying in a hospital bed. But as soon as that moment passed, her chest tightened. It was real—it was all real. Her legs radiated with pain, and her heart ached with the realization that she would never see her mother again.

"Good morning, hon," a middle-aged nurse said as she entered Cordelia's room, pushing a wheelchair. "How are you feeling today?"

Cordelia sniffed and brushed the tears from her cheeks.

The nurse gave her a look full of sadness. "It's okay to not be okay, honey. You've been through a lot."

"I'll be fine," Cordelia said quietly. "But my legs hurt."

"I'm sure they do," the nurse said as she walked toward Cordelia's bed. "I'm going to give you some more meds in your IV before we get you dressed and heading home. We'll send pain meds home with you, too."

"Thank you," Cordelia whispered, wiping tears.

They heard a light knock, and Salvatore's face appeared at her door.

"Morning," he croaked, clearing his throat. "Can I come in?"

"Yes, I was giving Cordelia some medication before we let you take her home," the nurse said.

Salvatore made his way into the room with one of Cordelia's duffle bags. His black suit was wrinkled and his face unshaven; his eyes were red from exhaustion. Cordelia hadn't seen him in a few days. Even though she was happy to see him, she was upset that he hadn't come sooner. Standing next her bed, he reached down and squeezed her hand.

"I brought you some clothes for the funeral," he said in a solemn voice. He opened the duffle bag, revealing a formal black dress.

A lump formed in Cordelia's throat, and she struggled to maintain her composure.

"Where have you been?" Cordelia asked with a hint of irritation in her voice.

"I'm sorry," Salvatore said, dropping his head.

The nurse awkwardly stood next to the bed while Cordelia bit her bottom lip.

Breaking the silence, the nurse said, "I can help you take a sponge bath and change into your clothes, hon."

Cordelia nodded weakly. She dreaded going to the funeral and saying her last goodbye. It felt like she was traveling down a one-way road where she couldn't turn back.

"I'll give you some privacy," Salvatore said as he walked out of the room.

With help from the nurse, Cordelia painfully lifted herself out of the bed and swiveled into the wheelchair. Her knees wobbled and her hands shook as she held onto the bed railing. The nurse went to the bathroom and turned on the faucets.

"When you're ready, I'll help you undress," the nurse said.

Feeling uncomfortable, Cordelia stared at the nurse for a moment. She had never undressed in front of a stranger before.

"Don't be nervous. I know it seems weird, but I do this all the time. I'm here to help," the nurse said. She gave Cordelia a reassuring smile and wheeled her toward the tiled bathroom.

Swallowing her discomfort and with the help of the kind nurse, Cordelia took a sponge bath, changed, and made it back to the hospital bed.

"Rest for a bit while I help your father with the discharge paperwork so you can go home," the nurse suggested, touching Cordelia's forearm. "If you need anything, hit the call button."

Cordelia nodded and within minutes, dozed off.

~

"All right, honey, are you ready to go?" Salvatore asked, gently waking her up.

Cordelia's eyes fluttered open. She nodded even though she didn't want to leave the nurse's care.

The nurse wheeled Cordelia through the hospital to the entrance, with Salvatore at her side.

"Make sure to keep your legs elevated as much as you can. If you need to get around, use the wheelchair until you start physical therapy," the nurse told her.

"Okay," Cordelia responded. "Thank you for everything."

"You're welcome," the nurse said. "Work hard and get better, okay?"

"I will," Cordelia replied.

Salvatore helped Cordelia into the car.

As her father drove to the cemetery, Cordelia stared at the side mirror, watching the hospital grew smaller.

"I'm so sorry I didn't come sooner," Salvatore apologized. "I've been lost the last few days. I've been stressed out and overwhelmed by all the funeral arrangements."

"It's okay, Dad," she lied. Her voice was tense when she added, "Grandpa was there for me."

Salvatore rubbed his forehead, his face paling even more.

~

Salvatore parked the car behind a black hearse and helped Cordelia into her wheelchair. They made their way up the sidewalk toward a grassy knoll. All of the circus performers and her grandfather were dressed in black. Tears welled up in Cordelia's eyes. A preacher stood next to her mother's casket which was draped with white tulips, her mom's favorite flower.

"Hi honey," Albert said as they approached. "Are your legs feeling better today?"

"A little better," Cordelia whispered. She wasn't okay, but what else was she supposed to say?

Several of the other circus performers approached Cordelia and gave her a hug.

"Shall we begin?" the preacher asked.

Everyone formed a loose half-circle around the casket as the preacher gave a short sermon and said a few prayers. Cordelia didn't pay much attention to him. To ease her grief, she tried closing her eyes, but scenes from the accident replayed in her mind. She reopened her eyes, stared at the casket, and whimpered.

After the service, all of the circus performers shook Salvatore's hand and patted him on the shoulder as they left. Paula stopped and gave Cordelia a hug. Cordelia stared at the ground until only her dad, her grandpa, and she remained.

"Dad, Cordelia and I need a few minutes alone. We'll meet you back at the cabin," Salvatore said.

Albert nodded and kissed Cordelia's forehead.

When he was out of sight, Salvatore stood next to Cordelia's wheelchair. He leaned down and gave her a long hug.

"I failed you, your mom, and everyone," he whispered as he pulled out the pocket watch.

"Dad, what are you doing?" Cordelia asked with fear in her voice.

"I can't live without your mother. It's too painful," he said.

Devastated, she thought *What about me? What about living for me?*

Swinging the watch back and forth, Salvatore whispered, "Time, erase my sadness.... Erase my tears... Erase my grief..."

His brown eyes faded into black coals, and his fists clenched. He stumbled forward and collapsed onto his knees.

"Dad!" Cordelia yelled.

She tried getting out of the wheelchair, but the pain kept her planted in the seat. She bent forward and rested her hands on her father's shoulder.

"Dad! Are you okay?" she cried.

She felt his warm skin turn cold, despite the suit coat he wore. He coughed a few times before looking up at Cordelia with a blank, dark stare.

"I'm fine," he said.

Something had changed. He picked himself up off the ground, brushed off his pants, and straightened his tie as though nothing was wrong.

"Let's go home," he said in a robotic tone without a hint of remorse. "No sense in wasting any more time here."

Cordelia stared at him with her mouth slightly open. *Wasting time!? How is this ever a waste of time!? What did he do?*

Grabbing the handles on her wheelchair, he silently pushed her to the car. As they drove back to the cabin in Siren Bay, Cordelia felt devastated, and her mind raced with too many questions.

⁓

"Stay here," Salvatore said coldly. He stormed into the cabin without knocking and slammed the door behind him.

She sat outside the cabin and wondered, *What's going on? Why did he leave me outside? Why is he being so quiet and mean?*

She struggled to hear their conversation through an open window.

"I'm leaving Cordelia with you," Salvatore said.

"What do you mean?" Albert said with surprise and concern in his voice. "Where are you going? What's going on?"

"I need to clear my head, so I'm leaving. You can be her guardian while I'm gone," Salvatore said.

What!? Cordelia screamed inside. It felt like her dad had stabbed her heart. *Take over guardianship? Why!?*

"What?" Albert raised his voice. "Who's going to take her to school in the winter? Traveling in a circus is no place for a teenager."

Salvatore's voice grew louder, "I was raised in the circus!"

"You always remind me how much you resented it. How you

missed having a normal childhood. How you had to make friends in every new city we lived in," Albert shot back.

"At this point it doesn't matter, and I don't care," Salvatore yelled.

My dad doesn't care about me anymore?! Cordelia's heart shattered.

Salvatore burst from the cabin, stomped past her without saying a word, and jumped into the rental car. The car tires squealed as Albert ran to Cordelia's side.

"He's changed," Albert said, shaking his head.

Her body trembled.

"What happened after I left the cemetery?" he asked, looking down at her.

"He asked the pocket watch to take away his sadness," she whimpered.

In shock, Albert sank to his knees and held her. Burying her head in his arms, she cried.

"He must've erased his ability to feel empathy," he whispered.

17

~

Mid-October

The cold leather cushion under her shoulders squeaked when Cordelia adjusted her position on the floor. She felt as though everyone was staring at her like a fish in an aquarium. Her spine lay flat on a floor mat in a room full of patients working with physical therapists on gym equipment.

"One leg at a time," Kurt, her therapist, instructed as he lifted each leg into the air and alternately bent them at the knees.

Biting her bottom lip, Cordelia stared at the ceiling. The fluorescent lights were too bright, and she clenched her eyes shut. She whimpered, prompting Kurt to lower her legs.

A burning question lingered in the back of her mind.

"Will I ever compete in the Olympics?"

"Perhaps," Kurt responded. "It all depends on how fast you heal and regain your strength, but you have to put a ton of effort into your therapy. It won't be easy."

~

Albert parked his truck in front of Siren Bay High School while Cordelia stared out the passenger window. Butterflies fluttered in her stomach at the thought of seeing her friends again. They would have a ton of questions about the accident, and she didn't know how to respond.

She opened the truck door, and Albert helped her slide out. Albert grabbed her backpack from the bed of the truck and handed it to her.

"Do you need help with your books or walking to class?" he asked.

She shook her head.

"Call me if you need anything. If you feel tired, I'll come pick you up."

She nodded as she slung the backpack over her shoulder. Dull pain shot through her knees as she limped down the sidewalk leading up to the main entrance.

Several students stared at her as she walked down the hall. Embarrassed, she avoided any eye contact. She stopped by her locker and dropped off her books.

A familiar voice called her name. She turned and saw Marcel standing behind her. He looked down at her legs and his face turned pale.

"I heard about the accident on the news," Marcel uttered in a solemn tone. "I'm sorry about what happened to you and your mom."

Cordelia stared at the floor, unable to respond right away.

"And I'm sorry I was such a jerk before," he continued. "I never should've blamed you. Can you forgive me?"

She looked up and said, "Yes, I forgive you."

He smiled.

After a few awkward minutes of silence, he said, "Well, I'll talk to you later."

"Okay, I would like that," she responded.

As Marcel turned and walked away, Cordelia saw Coach John standing in the doorway of his classroom.

"I didn't see you standing there," she blurted out.

Coach John walked over to her locker and said, "I'm so sorry to hear about the loss of your mom."

"It has been a rough few months," Cordelia responded, choking back her feelings.

"I bet," Coach said, glancing down at her legs. "I'm glad you're able to walk again."

"Me too," she said.

"How strong are your legs?" he asked. "Are you still in any pain?"

"Sometimes my knees hurt when I stand for too long," she replied.

"When do you think you'll be back in the pool?" Coach asked, raising his eyebrows. "Swimming should speed up your recovery."

"My legs are feeling stronger, but my physical therapist said it would be awhile before I can swim in a competition."

"Well, when you're ready, we'll get you back in the pool," Coach said, rubbing his forehead. "I'll get you back in shape."

"Thank you."

"You're welcome," he said with a smile. "I don't want to scare you, but I received a call from the Olympic officials."

A knot formed in her stomach knowing that her dreams teetered on the brink of failure.

"What did they say?" Cordelia asked.

"They didn't cut you from the team, and they're giving you some time to recover. In the spring, an official will come out to evaluate your progress and determine if you're still qualified."

With her chin held high, she felt a ray of hope. She promised herself that she wouldn't give up.

18

~

April 15th

After a long day at school, Cordelia elevated her legs with a pillow and wrapped an ice pack around her knees. While lying in bed, she overheard her grandpa in the living room, talking on the phone.

"Thanks, Paula, for running the circus while I take care of Cordelia. I know it's a lot of work, but I had no choice. You and Rego have been a tremendous help."

Albert paused for a moment and then replied, "Cordelia is doing better; she is no longer using crutches. By the way, how's Florida?"

He paused again before replying, "Glad you're enjoying the warm weather, it's still chilly here. We'll see you in a few weeks...Bye."

Her grandpa hung up the phone and let out a long sigh.

"Cordelia!" he shouted from the living room. "Dinner is ready. Do you need any help?"

"No, I got it," she replied.

She removed the ice pack and wrapped her knees with braces. She limped to the kitchen and sat down at the table. Before they could eat their meal, there was a knock on the cabin door.

Who could that it be? she wondered.

Albert walked over to the door and opened it. Detective Loch stood outside with a white envelope stuffed in his shirt pocket.

"Hello! Could I come in?" he asked. "I have good news for you."

"Sure, make yourself at home," Albert welcomed the officer. "Please, have a seat."

The detective sat down in a chair next to Cordelia.

"Sorry to interrupt your dinner, but I wanted to personally thank you for helping us solve the case," Loch apologized. "Rio and Murphy have been on the FBI's most wanted list for a long time."

"Really?" Albert responded, raising his eyebrows.

"Yes, but that's not the good news," Loch announced, sliding a white envelope across the table. "There was reward money for information leading to their arrest."

Albert opened up the envelope, pulled out a check, and his eyes popped. He turned the check around so Cordelia could see the number: $100,000.00.

"Wow," she whispered; her heart skipped a beat.

"Thank you!" Albert beamed.

"You deserve it for all your hard work," Loch responded. "I'm not sure how you knew where to find them, but I'm happy they're behind bars."

Cordelia knew they needed to keep the crystal ball a secret. Besides, the police would never believe their crazy story.

Looking at Cordelia, Loch said, "I heard you're testifying against Viktor at his trial tomorrow."

"Yes," she replied. "I'm nervous."

"I'll be there to support you," Albert reassured her.

Cordelia smiled.

"Good luck tomorrow. If you need anything, you can call me anytime," Loch said, sliding his business card across the table. He stood up from the table and shook Albert's and Cordelia's hands. "Well, I'll let you enjoy your dinner. Take care."

～

Cordelia sat in the witness stand, nervously looking around the courtroom. Two bailiffs stood in front of the judge's bench. The jury sat to her left, and the prosecuting attorney paced the floor in front of her.

Viktor sat next to his lawyer, giving Cordelia an angry stare.

"Please explain for the jury how you were kidnapped and by whom," the prosecutor inquired in a diplomatic tone.

"Rio and Murphy came to my family's circus to steal a scroll that I found in Lake Michigan," Cordelia explained. "When I told them I didn't have it, they took me hostage and brought me to a cabin in Mystique. Rio called Viktor, and I heard them talking on the phone about how Viktor planned the whole thing."

Viktor clenched his hands into a fist and gritted his teeth. He leaned over and whispered into his attorney's ear.

The attorney jumped up from his seat and declared, "Objection your honor, hearsay."

"Overruled," the judge said.

The prosecutor walked over to the evidence box on his table and pulled out the skeleton key.

Oh no! Why did he bring the key?! Gasping in horror, Cordelia fidgeted in her seat.

Before she could warn them, the prosecutor turned to Cordelia and asked, "Did you see the defendant point this key at the police in a threatening manner?"

As he stepped toward the witness stand, he stumbled, dropping the key to the floor.

Viktor lunged from his chair.

The sudden outburst frightened Cordelia and the jury. Albert jumped from his seat, ready to defend Cordelia.

Viktor snatched the key off the floor and pointed it at the two bailiffs. Thunder rumbled outside, and the overhead lights flickered. The two bailiffs drew their guns and pointed them at Viktor as the courtroom broke into chaos.

19

~

Viktor waved the key in the air.

BOOM!

A lightning bolt shot from the tip of the key and blew a gaping hole through the ceiling. The walls, floor, and ceiling shook as if there were an earthquake. The officers fell backwards, stunned by the shock wave. Chunks of ceiling fell on the bailiffs, pinning them to the ground.

The jury fell to their hands and knees. Cordelia ducked behind the judge's bench. The lawyers took cover under the tables while Albert ran to Cordelia's side.

Lightning bolts sprang from the tip of the key, destroying tables, chairs, and the witness stand. Sparks flew everywhere, catching the carpet on fire. Smoke filled the room, causing everyone to cough. The judge jumped from his seat, grabbed a nearby fire extinguisher, and fought the blaze. The lights went out, and the courtroom turned pitch black. The sound of shuffling feet and the chatter of the jury grew louder.

After a few moments, the lights came back on. Everyone looked around in a state of shock when Viktor was nowhere to be seen.

He escaped! Cordelia screamed inside, struggling to catch her breath.

Paramedics tended to the bailiffs while several police officers surveyed the damage in the courtroom and took statements from all of the witnesses. One officer approached Albert and Cordelia.

"Our team is searching the city. It's just a matter of time before we catch Viktor," the officer reassured them.

"What if he finds out where we live?" Albert asked.

"We'll patrol your neighborhood and keep a close eye on your home."

"Grandpa, what about tomorrow? I'll be at the YMCA for hours because the Olympic official is coming," Cordelia interjected. "They want to test my current time."

Looking at the officer, Albert asked, "Can you send a police officer to the YMCA? She's qualifying for the Olympics tomorrow."

"We can't offer twenty-four-hour protection, but we'll increase our patrols around the area." the officer promised. "Good luck with your qualifications, young lady."

"Thanks," Cordelia responded.

She had a sinking feeling in her stomach. She feared Viktor could show up at any moment. Now, more than ever, Viktor needed the scroll to escape from going to prison.

20

~

Cordelia sat on a bench in the girls' locker room. As she removed the brace, she noticed Ariel staring at her. She felt awkward as she glanced down at her legs. The scars were a painful reminder of the car accident.

"What are you staring at?" Cordelia demanded.

Ariel blushed and walked away.

Cordelia reached into her gym bag and pulled out her swimsuit. Feeling lightheaded, a flood of emotions resurfaced. To her, the swimsuit symbolized a final gift from her mom and the day her father left. Every time she wore it she felt the power of the Secret Talent Scroll, but her legs and heart would never work the same.

~

Cordelia adjusted her swim goggles and stood on the diving block. To calm her nerves, she used a breathing technique she learned from her coach. She looked over at the Olympic official wearing a button-down blouse, dress pants, and black-rimmed glasses. The official held a pen and clipboard in her hands while Coach John stood next to her, biting his nails.

BEEP!

The starter signal rang.

Cordelia leaped off the block and dove into the pool with her hands above her head in a streamlined position. A tingling sensation pulsated through her bathing suit as the Secret Talent Scroll's power worked its magic. Rotating her body to the surface, she inhaled through her mouth. As she reached the end of the pool her leg muscles tightened into a knot. A sharp pain ran through her calf muscles and she stopped mid-stroke. She grabbed her leg and sank to the bottom of the pool. Feeling the pressure build up in her lungs, she tried to massage her leg, but the pain was too great.

After a few minutes, Coach John jumped into the pool, pulled her out, and laid her on the concrete. Feeling defeated, she slammed her fist on the floor. The Olympic official walked toward them, scribbling some notes on her clipboard.

"This normally doesn't happen," Coach John came to Cordelia's defense. "Her time is improving."

"I had a leg cramp," Cordelia interjected.

"We can massage the muscles and try again," Coach John suggested.

"What is her current swim time for the hundred-meter freestyle?" the official asked.

"After the accident, her average time is fifty-seven seconds," her coach replied.

"Unfortunately, her time needs to improve in order to qualify. I'm sorry, but we have a replacement swimmer to fill her position. We'll definitely consider her in the future," the Olympic official said in a firm tone.

The words hit Cordelia hard. Her shoulders drooped as she stood up.

Wobbling on her weak legs, Cordelia looked at Coach John and asked, "Who's my replacement?"

"Ariel," he replied, looking at the floor.

In pain, Cordelia limped out of the pool area and into the hall. She cursed her predicament. Her senior year was supposed to be fun; instead she felt depressed. Her whole world unraveled before her eyes. She leaned against the wall, covered her face with her hands, and screamed.

As tears streamed down her cheeks, she felt a warm hand on her shoulder.

"Go away! I don't want to talk right now," she stuttered.

"What's wrong?"

She dropped her hands. Through blurry eyes she saw Marcel standing in front of her.

"I was disqualified from the Olympics!"

"I'm sorry. I understand how you feel," Marcel responded.

She shook her head.

"I worked for seven years learning how to swim faster," she poured out her frustration. "All that work was for nothing. I deserve to win. I deserve money from endorsement deals. It's all gone!"

"You think I didn't work hard, too?!" Marcel shot back. "While you were in the pool, I was in the gym working out and building my muscles. I lost it all, too!"

"You're right," she said as she tried to calm her emotions.

In that moment, they both carried the same agony.

"What am I going to do now?" she asked.

"I'm still figuring that out myself," he said, shrugging his shoulders. "Do you need a ride home?"

"My grandpa is supposed to pick me up, but I can call him," she said, her cheeks reddening slightly. "I'll tell him you'll bring me home instead."

~

The sky grew dark, and storm clouds formed overhead as Marcel's car rolled down the long driveway toward Cordelia's cabin. A flash of light was followed by a gigantic boom that shook the car. A lightning bolt struck the hood, scorching it black. Steam rolled out from underneath the hood. Marcel slammed on the brakes, and the car came to a stop.

"What's going on?" Marcel asked with stress in his voice. "And who's that?"

Viktor stood on the front lawn, pointing the skeleton key at them.

"Oh no! It's Viktor!" Cordelia yelled. "He wants the Secret Talent Scroll back. He has the power to control lightning."

"Like Zeus?" Marcel asked with a stunned look.

"Yeah, sort of," Cordelia urgently responded. "Get down!"

They ducked as lightning grazed the top of the car. A thunderous boom made her ears ring. Heat radiated through the metal, melting the fabric on the car's ceiling.

21

~

"Stay down!" Marcel commanded. "I'll protect you."

Marcel jumped out of the car and popped the trunk. He pumped the 50-pound dumbbells, and his muscles expanded, and his stature grew six inches. His shirt ripped as his biceps bulged. He grabbed a tire iron and ripped the trunk hood off its hinges. He held the tire iron like a sword and the hood like a shield.

Cordelia opened the door and hid behind the car. She peered over the roof. Albert stood on the front porch of the cabin, beckoning her.

"Cordelia, run!" Marcel exclaimed as he ran toward Viktor, providing cover while Cordelia ran to her grandfather's side.

Viktor waved the key in the air. Storm clouds rumbled as lightning jumped from the key and struck Marcel's shield, causing sparks to fly everywhere. Marcel fell to the ground and dropped his shield. His arm twitched as he yelped in pain.

Viktor pointed the key at Marcel.

"Watch out!" Cordelia warned him.

Marcel rolled over as another lightning bolt struck the lawn next to him, catching the grass on fire.

Viktor pointed the key at a tall oak tree in the front yard, and a lightning bolt split the tree into two pieces. Splinters flew everywhere as a giant branch crashed down on Marcel, pinned him to the ground, and the leaves draped over his body.

Cordelia and Albert ducked inside the house and locked the door behind them. Her grandpa ran to his bedroom to fetch the scroll.

Her heart raced, and her hands trembled as she dialed 911.

"Hello!" She cried. "Could you send the police?"

She frantically explained the situation and gave the dispatcher her address.

Holding up the scroll, Albert exclaimed, "Got it!"

Cordelia hung up the phone and followed Albert back outside.

The heavy branch rolled off Marcel's back as he stood up. He threw the tree limb, striking Viktor in the arm. The key flew out of his hand and landed several feet away. Marcel ran over to Viktor, pushed him to the ground, and held him down with his foot.

Reading from the scroll, Albert chanted, "I call upon the four classical elements: wind, fire, earth and water. Wind moves sand. Fire creates earth and ash. Earth absorbs water. Water quenches fire. Remove the electrical power given to Viktor and his key."

The wind subsided and the storm clouds disappeared. The glowing orange tip of the key faded while the metal turned cold. Marcel slowly shrank down to a normal-size human again.

"No!" Viktor groaned, clutching his broken arm.

Sirens echoed through the trees while blue and red lights reflected off the cabin windows. Cordelia ran over to the key, picked it up, and put it her pocket. A police car pulled into the driveway and, with guns drawn, two officers jumped out of the car.

"You're under arrest," one officer shouted, pointing his pistol at Viktor.

Defeated, Viktor raised his hand in the air and surrendered while the officer read him his Miranda rights.

As the police led him away, Viktor shouted to Albert and Cordelia, "May the scroll curse you both!"

His words loomed over Cordelia like a dark storm cloud.

The police placed Viktor in the back of the car and locked the doors. While one officer filled out paperwork, the other officer walked over to Albert to gather information.

Cordelia ran to Marcel and asked, "Are you okay?"

"My back hurts," Marcel responded, breathing heavily.

As Marcel rubbed his back, Cordelia noticed a gash on his cheek.

"You're hurt," she said with concern. "Let me get you something for your cut."

She ran to the bathroom, grabbed some antiseptic, a cotton ball, and bandages. She rushed back to Marcel and tended to his wound.

"Ouch," Marcel said with a flinch as she cleaned his wound and placed a bandage on his cheek.

After several minutes, Albert finished talking with the police, and they took Viktor away.

Albert approached Marcel, extended his hand and exclaimed, "Thank you for saving us! You're a brave young man."

Cordelia nodded as Albert shook Marcel's hand.

"Thanks," Marcel responded. "I didn't want him to hurt Cordelia."

"Well, if you need anything," Albert said, "you can contact me anytime. I owe you a debt of gratitude."

"It was no problem," Marcel said.

"How did your muscles get so big?" Albert asked.

"Cordelia used the scroll to make my muscles grow bigger. It usually wears off after a while. I'm learning how to control it."

Albert stumbled backward in shock.

Looking at Cordelia, Albert asked, "You used the scroll without my knowledge?"

"I'm sorry," she replied, looking sheepishly at the ground.

"You shouldn't take risks like that, Cordelia," Albert scolded her. "We don't want the powers falling into the wrong hands. You should've thought things through."

"I know that now," Cordelia said with remorse.

Looking back at Marcel, Albert said, "But then again, you seem like a good kid."

"Thank you, sir," Marcel replied.

"You promise to do good in this world?" Albert asked.

"Yes, sir."

"Good," Albert said with a nod. "Well, it's getting late. We had a long day. Cordelia, why don't you say goodbye, and I'll meet you back in the house?"

Cordelia nodded.

As Albert walked back to the cabin, she escorted Marcel to his car.

"I hope it starts," Marcel grunted. "Otherwise, I'll need to call a tow truck."

"If it doesn't, my grandpa can take you home," Cordelia said. "Thanks for defending me. And thanks for the ride home."

"Anytime," he replied.

As they stood next to his car, Cordelia reached up and gave him a hug. She felt his burly chest and strong arms wrap around her tiny frame. He gently squeezed her, restraining the full power of his muscles. She felt protected by his strength and presence. After few moments, he let go and stepped backwards, closer to his car.

Unsure what else to say next, she smiled and looked down. It felt like he was going to say something, but he just rubbed the back of his head and smiled. He hopped into the car, rolled down the window, and started it. It cranked over a few times before it sputtered to life. Marcel wiped his brow and let out a sigh of relief. He stared into her eyes for a brief moment.

"Can we go out some time?" he asked.

"I would like that," she responded with a wide smile, her heart skipping a beat.

"Awesome," he replied.

As Marcel drove away, he stuck his arm out the car window and waved.

~

Cordelia went to her bedroom and hid the skeleton key in a dresser drawer. Plopping down on her bed, she rested her head on the pillow.

Albert knocked on the bedroom door, "Can I come in?"

"Yes."

He entered the room, sat down on the bed next to Cordelia, and said warmly, "I wanted to check in on you. We had a crazy few days. If you need to talk about it, I'm here."

"My heart is going a hundred miles an hour!" she replied. "Hopefully, I can sleep tonight."

"Well, it's all over. Viktor won't be bothering us anymore."

"What if Viktor is right?" Cordelia speculated. "What if we're cursed by the scroll?"

"Don't worry, the past is behind us, and the spell is broken," Albert reassured her. "He can't use the key anymore. We can move forward without fear."

For a brief moment, Cordelia felt relaxed, but then her thoughts shifted back to her Olympic dreams. She rolled over, buried her head in the pillows, and rocked back and forth.

"What's wrong?" Albert asked with concern.

"I was cut from the Olympic Swim Team. They already found a replacement," she replied, her bottom lip quivering.

"Your coach told me you've been making progress. You've come so far in your recovery, don't they see that?"

"Yes, but my time needs to be better to qualify," she angrily responded.

"I know you're feeling terrible, and I've noticed how sad you've been. We had a rough year," he said with a sigh. "So, I planned a full day of fun on Sunday."

"Where are we going?" she asked, looking up at her grandpa.

"It's a surprise," he replied.

22

~

Standing in line behind a few theater goers, Cordelia read the marquee over the Howmet Playhouse: *Alice in Wonderland*.

Albert reached into his coat pocket, pulled out his camera, and tapped his fingers on the shoulder of a woman standing in front of him.

"Excuse me, could you take a picture of my granddaughter and me?" Albert asked.

"Sure," the woman replied.

The woman took Albert's camera, stepped back, and lined up the shot while Albert put his arm around Cordelia and smiled. Out of the corner of her eye, Cordelia noticed a young boy riding his bike down the sidewalk straight toward them. He was looking down at the ground instead of paying attention.

As the woman snapped the picture, the boy looked up and lost control of his bike. He crashed right next to Cordelia. By some sheer accident, he was forever captured in the photograph.

Albert helped the boy off the ground while Cordelia picked up the bike.

"Are you okay?" Albert asked with concern.

The boy's face turned beet red. He was a tall, skinny boy with blonde hair and appeared to be a few years younger than Cordelia.

"Yes, sir," the boy stuttered.

"What's your name, son?" Albert asked.

"Flynn Parkes," the boy replied, avoiding eye contact.

"Well, be careful riding home, Flynn," Albert said.

Flynn nodded, hopped on his bike, and peddled down the sidewalk.

Albert scratched his head and looked at Cordelia. A butterfly flew down from a nearby tree and landed on her shoulder. The butterfly flapped its wings for a few moments before it flew away.

"It must be a sign of good luck!" Albert speculated.

Cordelia shrugged her shoulders and smiled halfheartedly. She wasn't feeling lucky.

～

After the play, the audience stood up and clapped while Cordelia sat in her seat. The play might have been a hit with the audience, but it was a minor distraction from her problems. Her mind fell back into darkness.

Cordelia looked over at her grandpa and cracked a small smile. "Thanks Grandpa, I had fun."

"I have more things planned," Albert replied with a wink.

"Where are we going now?" she asked.

"You'll see," he replied.

～

Albert's pick-up truck pulled into the driveway of the Double Tree Ranch in Rothbury, Michigan. There were two large red barns, several horses grazing in an open field, and a fenced-in area with wood bleachers along the edges. Albert found an empty parking spot next to a sign announcing a rodeo show. As Cordelia trudged through the field toward the main entrance, her shoes became muddy. She felt out of place as hordes of people dressed in cowboy hats, boots, and jeans gathered for the event.

A pair of rodeo clowns entertained the crowd near the ticket booth. Albert and Cordelia stopped for a moment and watched the show. One rodeo clown twirled a lasso in a clockwise motion. As he pulled the rope toward his body, he skipped back and forth through the hoop while the other clown created balloon a animal in the shape of a bull with horns.

"They're pretty good," Albert remarked.

Cordelia nodded.

The audience clapped at the end of show as the clowns took a bow and gathered their props. As they walked away, Cordelia noticed the names "Sammy" and "Buster" stitched in black letters on the backs of their shirts.

~

Standing next to the wood fence, Cordelia and Albert watched the rodeo. A cowboy gave a nod to the judges to start the clock. The gate burst open, and a bull stormed out of the chute box and into the large field. The angry beast kicked and bucked as the bull rider's left arm flailed the air. His right hand kept a firm grip on the rope wrapped around the bull's torso and underbelly. Within a few seconds, the bull bucked the cowboy off its back, and the rider fell to the ground in a cloud of dust. He stood up, brushed the dirt off his jeans, and straightened his cowboy hat while Sammy and Buster ran into the action and distracted the bull. The cowboy picked up a stone and spit on the ground. He hurled the rock, hitting the bull's snout. The bull kicked his hind legs, striking Sammy in the shin. Sammy buckled in pain and grabbed his leg. Another cowboy on a horse herded the bull back into the chute.

Buster's face turned bright red as he ran toward the bull rider with his fists raised to his shoulders. The cowboy shouted, but Cordelia couldn't decipher his words. He pushed Buster backwards, and the crowd jeered. One of the officials ran into the ring and broke up the fight. After arguing for a few minutes, the official pointed to the parking lot. Buster shook his head and stomped out of the arena as Sammy chased after him.

When they passed by Cordelia, she overheard their

conversation.

"Buster, what happened?"

"I got fired!"

"But, the cowboy threw a rock at the bull. He should've been disqualified."

"Apparently, the judges didn't see it," Buster replied, pulling his car keys out of his pocket. "We don't need this place!"

Albert cleared his throat and approached the two men. Cordelia followed his lead.

"Excuse me, gentleman," Albert interjected.

The two men stopped, turned around, and looked Albert up and down.

"My name is Albert Da Vinci and this is my granddaughter, Cordelia. I'm the owner of a traveling circus. We've been watching your routine, and you guys are talented."

"Thanks," Buster replied.

"Currently we don't have any clowns," Albert explained. "I would like to expand our circus to include more performers."

Sammy scratched his head, "Do you want to hire us?"

"Stop by tomorrow morning, and we'll talk," Albert said, handing them a business card with his phone number and home address.

Buster shook Albert's hand and replied, "Okay, see you soon."

Sammy and Buster waved goodbye as they jumped into their car and drove off.

Cordelia admired her grandpa's willingness to help people by giving everyone a chance.

Albert turned to Cordelia and apologized, "Sorry about that. I thought we could use some new talent."

She nodded.

"Are you having fun yet?" he asked with a hopeful smile.

She shrugged her shoulders and looked down at the ground. She wanted to feel happy, but she couldn't fake her feelings no matter how hard she tried. When she looked up, she noticed his eyes begin to water.

"Okay, we can go," he said, his shoulders slumped.

∽

Instead of driving to their cabin in Siren Bay, they traveled south on US 31 and then turned west toward Lake Michigan.

Are we taking the long way home? Cordelia wondered.

Driving along Scenic Drive, Albert's elbow rested on the truck's window ledge while his hand cradled his forehead. He pulled to the side of the road before the bridge spanning the Duck Lake Channel.

The sun began to set, turning the blue sky into an orange and purple blur. Beyond the rolling sand dunes, Cordelia saw the shoreline of Lake Michigan.

Albert opened the truck door and grabbed a brown duffle bag from the bed of his truck.

"Let's take a walk along the beach so we can talk," he said.

23
~

The beach was empty as most of the tourists and locals had gone home. A flock of seagulls took flight as they walked along the beach, and a light breeze gave Cordelia goose bumps. Albert picked up a smooth blue stone and threw it into the water. It skipped a few times before sinking into the lake.

"This is a sink-or-swim moment," he muttered under his breath.

"Huh? What do you mean, Grandpa?" Cordelia asked. She was baffled; was he talking to her or to himself?

He placed his arm around her shoulders and stared out over Lake Michigan without answering her. The spectacular view seemed to go on forever with no land in sight, even though she knew Milwaukee was straight across the lake 90 miles away. The sound of waves crashing onto the beach sent shivers down her spine. The stress drained from her body, and she felt happy sharing this quiet moment with her grandpa.

"I need to talk to you about something very important," Albert whispered.

They sat down on the beach, facing each other.

He gently took her hand and said, "I searched the crystal ball. I saw your dad coming home."

"Dad is coming home!? When?"

A tear of joy trickled down her cheek. At least she knew he wouldn't be gone forever. However, even though she missed him, she was still angry at him for leaving her. He left without even saying goodbye and that hurt more than she could ever explain.

"Yes, your father will come home. But I can't tell exactly when or where," her grandpa said. He paused and took a breath. "I also saw you competing in the Olympics."

"What!?" Cordelia almost jumped up with surprise. "Are you serious? Me!? I will swim in the Olympics!?" Her voice was higher than normal, her eyes bulging.

Albert smiled. "Yes, honey, it's true."

"But... How?" Cordelia's spirit soared, but her rational mind settled back in. "With my legs... How?"

"I will show you," Albert said. He reached into the duffle bag and pulled out the crystal ball. He waved his hands over the ball and asked, "How can I help Cordelia become an Olympic swimmer?"

The core of the ball glowed bright amber, and purple smoke swirled inside. An expanding universe seemed to be trapped inside the crystal ball with images flickering like a tiny 3D movie screen. First, it showed Albert and Cordelia walking along the beach, followed by Albert reading from the scroll, but then the images became blurry.

"What's happening?" Cordelia asked, squinting at the muddled images.

"I noticed that all of the images from the future are like distant ripples on a lake. As though time and space are in transition with each decision we make," her grandpa explained in a solemn tone. "What we see is a possible future, not a guarantee."

The images sped into the future where Cordelia appeared to be a few years older. She stood next to the swimming pool while the crowd cheered. She smiled and waved as the scoreboard flashed, "Cordelia Da Vinci: new Olympic record!" Her father was in the audience jumping up and down in celebration.

As the image faded, Cordelia's eyes widened with excitement.

"Should we give it a try?" Albert asked.

"Absolutely!" Cordelia responded.

He reached into the duffle bag and pulled out the swimsuit that her mother had made. He handed the suit to Cordelia. She ran up the sand dune and changed behind some bushes and trees while Albert prepared the Secret Talent Scroll.

Out of breath, she returned and sat beside her grandfather. She tried to remain calm, but she couldn't—she was too excited.

What if I become the fastest swimmer in the world? And then a negative voice crept back into her soul: *But what if it doesn't work? What if I live out the rest my life with the scars from the accident?* Her positive voice shouted back: *This will work!*

"I call upon the four classical elements: wind, fire, earth, and water," Albert chanted. "Wind moves sand. Fire creates earth and ash. Earth absorbs water. Water quenches fire. Heal Cordelia's legs so she can be the best swimmer in the world, again."

Storm clouds gathered in the sky, and a gust of wind created a tornado with the beach sand. A tiny lightning bolt struck the sand, creating pops and sparks like a mini fireworks show. The embers from the small explosion sprayed onto Cordelia's legs. She flinched out of instinct, but the sparks didn't hurt—they caused her skin to tingle.

A giant wave crashed on the shore and soaked their legs. When the water receded, a large salmon floundered in Cordelia's lap. The fish gasped for air and slapped its tail against her ankles. Cordelia fumbled to throw it back into the lake, but before she could, the fish melted into green molecules and wrapped around her feet like socks. She felt them seep into her skin and move through her bloodstream, like a fish swimming inside of her. Her tan legs turned a dark shade of green and fish scales began to protrude around her feet and toes. The scales spread across her skin from her ankles to her shins, stopping at her thighs. She watched in horror as the scales covered all of the scars from the car accident.

Stunned, Cordelia tried to kick her legs, but they wouldn't move. Her lips quivered and she cried out, "What's happening to me!?"

"I – I – I don't know!" Albert sputtered. He didn't move; he was glued to the sand.

"Grandpa, make it stop!" Cordelia screamed as her legs fused together, morphing into a mermaid's tail.

24

~

The storm clouds disappeared, and the moonlight reflected off Cordelia's tail, making it shimmer.

Albert repeated the spell over and over again, each time ending with, "Give Cordelia the ability to walk again."

Despite all his efforts, nothing changed. Was her fate sealed? Was she destined to be a mermaid, and for how long? She wanted her legs back, scars and all.

"Did you see this in the crystal ball?" she cried, her voice shaking.

"No!" he replied. "I didn't know this would happen. I'm sorry. I can't explain why all of the images from the future are blurry and the images from the past are crystal clear."

Her face turned red, and she slammed her fists on the sand.

"How could you do this to me?" she demanded.

Albert reached out and touched her hand, but she recoiled. His face turned pale.

"I wanted to make you happy! I hope you can forgive me," he pleaded.

"I'm not sure if I can forgive you," she responded, gritting her teeth.

"I thought the scroll would help you swim again. I never thought it would turn you into a mermaid!"

A tingling sensation ran through her tail, and her throat became dry. Gills opened underneath her jaw and she gasped for air. Her fish tail flopped on the beach as she pointed toward Lake Michigan.

Albert panicked. He gently lifted her off the sand, waded into the water, and set her down.

She clawed her way deeper into the lake as the waves crashed over her body. Water entered her gills and oxygen pumped through her arteries. Every little breath became a tiny little gift to her lungs. After her panic subsided, she allowed her mermaid body to function like a fish. She used her gills to stabilize her breathing and she used her tail to swim in the water.

She knew her grandpa loved her and that he was trying to fix things. Her anger dissipated and she wanted to make amends. She felt alone without her parents and she didn't want to lose her grandpa, too. Popping her head above the water, she scanned the beach. Albert stood knee-deep a hundred yards in front of her. She swam closer to him, giving him a weary smile.

"I'm sorry I got angry with you. I know you're only trying to help," she said sincerely. "What do we do now?"

"We wait and see if your legs turn back to normal. I won't leave you. I'll be right here," he reassured her.

"Okay," she said with a bit of relief.

Swimming faster than any human, she propelled her body through the lake using her newly formed tail. Like a swordfish under the pale light of the moon, she breached the crest of a wave and sailed into the air.

SPLASH!

She dove into the cold murky water. Disoriented, she crashed, bumping her head at the bottom of the lake and knocking herself unconscious. Her vision faded to black.

25

~

ordelia woke up in her warm bed. Everything was a blur, and she couldn't remember how she got home or what day of the week it was. A headache pounded in her skull, and she felt a painful lump on her forehead. She twitched her legs and wiggled her toes, but she was afraid to look under the covers. Everything felt normal, so she slowly slid out of the bed. Two scarred legs, two feet, and ten toes emerged from underneath the covers.

Maybe it was a nightmare, she thought, letting out a sigh of relief.

She stood up, limped to the bathroom, and took a shower.

After putting on some fresh clothes, she walked into the kitchen where Albert was pouring a cup of coffee. His hands trembled, his shoulders were hunched over, and his hair was a mess.

"Good morning, Grandpa," she said, still groggy.

He nearly jumped out of his skin. He yelped in pain as some of the coffee spilled onto his hands. He set the coffee cup on the countertop, grabbed a paper towel, and wiped the floor.

"Good morning, sweetie," he replied as he cleaned up the mess.

"What happened last night?"

"You don't remember?" he asked, rubbing his forehead.

"I had this crazy dream that I turned into a mermaid."

He sat in a chair, leaned back, and murmured, "It wasn't a dream."

Cordelia's face turned pale.

"The last thing I remember was you putting me into Lake Michigan," she said when she regained her composure. "What happened next?"

"You were in the water for several hours, and I began to worry because I hadn't seen you. I was afraid you might've drowned!" he replied with a quiver in his voice.

He stood up, paced the floor, and continued, "I walked up and down the beach scanning the waves for any sign of you. At daybreak, I found you lying on the beach about a mile and half north of Duck Lake Channel. You were sound asleep. I picked you up, brought you home, and tucked you into bed."

"But my legs, I have legs instead of a fish tail!"

"Maybe you turn into a mermaid at night. Or maybe the spell has been broken. Only time will tell."

Questions without answers made her feel anxious.

"I'm late for school!" she exclaimed.

"I called and I told them you were sick. You can stay home until we sort things out."

"This is horrible!" she complained. "What am I going to tell my friends? What if I'm like this forever? How will I ever get married or have kids?"

"I don't know," he replied, nervously tapping his foot on the floor.

Her mood fell into a dark hole of despair. Feeling angry, she wanted someone or something to blame. She cursed the Secret Talent Scroll and the crystal ball.

"What am I going to do now?" she asked.

"We'll figure something out," Albert tried to reassure her.

Am I ever going to be normal again? What if I'm like this forever? Her mind wandered, imagining all kinds of gloomy scenarios.

Knock, knock, knock!

"Who's here?" she asked.

"Oh no!" Albert sighed. "I told the rodeo clowns I would give them a job interview."

"Now?" Cordelia groaned.

She was annoyed by the interruption because she had a lot to discuss with her grandpa. She followed Albert to the door and peered over his shoulder.

Wearing everyday clothes, the two rodeo clowns from the Double Tree Ranch stood outside. They weren't wearing any clown makeup, and they appeared to be twins with the same squinty eyes and prominent ears.

"Hey guys," Albert said. "I forgot you were stopping by today. Things have been crazy."

"Hello, did we come at a bad time?" Sammy asked. "We should've called first."

Albert looked over at Cordelia and wavered for a moment before replying, "Yes, it's a bad time."

"No, it's okay, Grandpa." she interjected. "We can talk later."

"Are you sure?" Albert said, placing his hand on her shoulder.

She reluctantly nodded, hoping they wouldn't stay very long.

Albert looked back at Sammy and Buster, pointed to the couch in the living room, and said, "Please, come in and have a seat. Do you want something to drink, coffee or tea?"

"No, thank you," Buster replied as he sat down on the couch.

"I'm going to make some breakfast," Cordelia said, feeling a bit out of place.

"Okay, sweetie," Albert said.

She walked into the kitchen and poured herself a bowl of cereal. She knew that life kept going despite her own problems, but everything was happening so fast that she felt like she couldn't control her life anymore. She was afraid that if she went back to school she would turn into to a mermaid during class. *Will my friends think I'm a freak or accept me for who I am?* Her mind swirled with "what-ifs."

The kitchen was right next to the living room, so she could hear her grandpa's voice. She stopped contemplating her fate to listen in on their conversation.

"So, could you tell me a little about yourselves and your training?" Albert began.

"We're brothers," Sammy stated.

"I thought you two were related," Albert remarked.

"We've been rodeo clowns since high school," Sammy continued. "Our grandfather was a rodeo clown and vaudeville performer in Muskegon. He taught us all about the business."

"That's quite the family background," Albert said. "My crew tours the southern states during the winter. In the summer we travel all over Michigan. Would you be okay with that schedule?"

"Yes, sir," Sammy replied.

"Do you want to join the show?" Albert asked.

"When can we start?"

"My crew is touring in Florida for the winter," Albert replied. "They'll be back in two weeks, so you can start then."

"So, Buster, what do you think? Should we join the circus?"

"Sure, why not?" Buster replied.

"You're hired!" Albert declared. "We'll work on developing a first-class act for you."

"Thank you!" they said in unison.

After she heard them leave, Albert walked into the kitchen and sat down next to Cordelia.

"There are two spells on the scroll," Albert said. "One chant gives you magical powers, and the other reverses them."

"So, turn me back into a normal human," she interjected.

"I tried several times last night, but it didn't work. The scroll states that the spell can be broken only 'if the person uses the power for evil.' And you're a good person. You would never do anything bad."

"What do we do now?" she asked.

26

"Our top priority is finding a way to get you back to normal," Albert said. "However, breaking the spell could take some time."

Cordelia's anxiety increased. She wanted a quick solution, but she was at the mercy of time.

"When we travel this summer, we won't always be near a lake," Albert continued. "So, I had an idea. I'm buying you a camper with the reward money from the police. I made some phone calls this morning, and I found someone who can build an aquarium that will fit inside a large RV."

"You mean I can have my own camper?" she asked, feeling excited about having privacy.

"Yes," he responded.

"That would be awesome," she said, but she still had a hard time accepting her new reality.

"What do you think of my idea?" Albert asked.

"I like it," she replied. "I don't want anyone to find out my secret."

He wearily nodded.

Albert and Cordelia drove to the nearest RV dealership. The lot was filled with trailers, pop-up campers, motor homes, and everything in between. As they browsed the line of vehicles, a long pearl-colored camper with shiny wheel rims and tinted windows caught Cordelia's eye. She wandered over to it while Albert followed behind her.

A salesman approached her with a bright smile. He had slicked-back hair, and wore a windbreaker with a flipped-up collar.

"Do you want to take a look inside?" the salesman asked without missing a beat.

"Sure," Cordelia replied.

He opened the door, and she stepped inside the RV with Albert. They looked around the spacious interior. It had a bathroom, bedroom, living room, and a small kitchen.

"What do you think?" Albert asked.

"I love it!" Cordelia responded.

He looked at the salesman and said, "We'll take it."

~

Staring out her bedroom window, Cordelia worried about her future. She wondered how long the spell would last and if the crystal ball lied.

How will I ever compete in the Olympics if I'm a mermaid? she thought. *When will my dad come home? When will I turn back to normal?*

Feeling overwhelmed by her thoughts, she sat down on the edge of her bed with her journal and wrote a poem.

Cold water surrounded her body
While her warm heart remained strong.
A mermaid who no longer feared drowning;
Will she rise above the darkness
Or sink into the abyss?

Clanking hammers and the loud whine of a circular saw broke her concentration. She limped downstairs and into the living room of the cabin. Pushing back the curtains on the picture window, she saw two pick-up trucks with the words "Gainsborough Home Builders" written on the side. Parked next to her new RV was a white van covered in colorful fish decals and black lettering that read "Exotic Aquariums, Inc."

Albert emerged from the kitchen and asked, "Should we check on their progress?"

Cordelia nodded.

They stepped outside and walked a few yards to their new RV. Albert opened the door, and they climbed inside. The workers had removed a few walls and built a rectangular metal frame to hold the glass panels of the aquarium which was roughly the size of a small swimming pool.

"How's it going?" Albert asked.

The owner of the construction crew, Mr. Gainsborough, wiped his brow with a red handkerchief and replied, "Everything is going good. As long as we distribute the weight of the water and tank over the tires, I think you should be okay with the hauling capacity."

"How long do you think it will take?" Albert asked.

"If we don't run into any problems, we should have it done by this weekend," Mr. Gainsborough responded.

"Great."

After Albert made a partial payment for their work, the construction crew packed up their tools and drove home.

"Six o'clock," Albert said, looking at his watch. "Let's eat dinner before I take you back to Lake Michigan."

Cordelia's stomach grumbled as her anxiety grew.

～

Dreading the sunset, Cordelia lay in bed staring at the ceiling. Soon, she would be far away from the comfort of her home. She heard a knock on her bedroom door.

"Come in," she said.

With a duffle bag in his hand, Albert walked into the room and sat down on the edge of the bed.

"It's time to go," Albert said in a solemn tone. "Here's a duffle bag with a towel in it. You may want to pack some dry clothes."

"I don't want to do this," she said with tears in her eyes.

Her grandpa wrapped his arms around her. She wept, letting out all her frustrations in a flood of emotions.

When her sobs subsided, she wiped her cheeks and looked up at Albert.

"Whatever it takes to correct the past and regain your future, we'll do it together," Albert reassured her. "I'll help you find your life's purpose, even if you're turning into a mermaid."

27

~

The orange sun painted the sky with shades of red, and the clouds reflected off the waves pounding on the beach. Cordelia took off her sandals and dipped her toes into the cold, wet sand. A tingling sensation pulsated through her legs. Her face turned pale and her heart sank.

"It's happening again," she announced with dread.

"Are you sure?" Albert asked in an urgent whisper.

"Yes."

Feeling defeated by fate, Cordelia sat in the water as her legs fused together. Gasping for air, she panicked for a brief moment before rolling into the water and swimming till her lungs adjusted to her new surroundings and receiving oxygen from her gills. Popping her head above the water, she saw Albert roll out a sleeping bag and set a pillow on the beach. She swam close to him while he set up his makeshift camp. He climbed inside the sleeping bag and made himself comfortable.

Making eye contact with her, he said, "I'll watch over you tonight. Hopefully your aquarium will be ready soon so you can sleep at home. Be careful, and don't get lost."

"I won't get lost," Cordelia said with a chuckle.

"I love you," Albert said.

His words made her smile and warmed her heart.

"I love you too, Grandpa."

She felt lost without her mom or dad around. She knew her grandpa would watch over her tonight, but what happens when he passed away? She had to find a way to become independent and strong.

She sank underwater. Floating in the cold darkness, the ebb and flow of the waves soothed her nerves. She heard the fish swimming, currents shifting, and the waves crashing on the beach. Swimming away from the land, she felt free without the fear of drowning.

How can I overcome my problems? she thought. *How can I use my new talents? Where am I going, and who am I now?*

She created a pillow of sand, curled up on the bottom of the lake, and fell asleep with her thoughts.

～

Cordelia woke up and swam toward the beach as the sun rose above the horizon. She darted along the sandy bottom like a scuba diver exploring every crevice. A few Petoskey and Leelanau Blue stones caught her eye. She stopped, picked them up, and held them in her hand as a school of fish swam past her.

On shore, her fish tail slowly turned back into legs. She hid behind some bushes, dried off with a towel, changed into her dry clothes, and ran her fingers through her hair. Her grandpa rustled inside his sleeping bag. He stood up and rubbed his sleepy eyes. He rolled up his sleeping bag and tucked it under his arm.

He spotted Cordelia and said, "Morning, sweetie."

"Morning, Grandpa."

As they walked back to his pick-up truck, Albert said, "Sunrise is at seven a.m. that only gives you about hour to get ready for school. You'll need to be home before eight twenty-eight p.m. for sunset. So, you'll have an early curfew. That'll limit your after-school activities."

Cordelia stared down the shoreline, mulling over her new schedule.

"That stinks," she said.

"Do you think you're ready to go back to school?" Albert asked.

Cordelia let out a sigh and bit a fingernail. *What if someone finds out my secret?*

"I don't want to rush you, but you can't miss any more school," Albert said. "You missed a lot of classes because of the car accident, and you might not have enough credits to graduate this year."

"I know; you're right," she bitterly responded.

"What are you thinking?" Albert asked.

"I'm scared of what people might say," she responded. "But I do want to go back to school."

"Are you sure you're ready?" he asked.

She thought for a few moments before reluctantly nodding.

"Okay," Albert said.

~

8 a.m. Siren Bay High School

"Are you feeling okay?" Marcel asked. "I didn't see you at school yesterday."

Cordelia's heartbeat quickened, and her face reddened. She closed her locker door and turned around.

"I'm okay," she responded, holding her books close to her chest. "I've been sick."

She deflected his question because she didn't want to reveal her secret.

"Are you feeling better now?" Marcel asked.

"Yeah... I'm okay," Cordelia responded. She figured if she kept her responses short then she wouldn't have to explain herself.

"Good..." They stood in silence for a few seconds before Marcel cleared his throat and continued, "Hey, so, I know this is short notice, but do you want to go to the prom with me?"

28

~

Cordelia wanted to say yes, but she hesitated to answer Marcel's question. Her excitement was dampened by her new reality.

Breaking the awkward silence, Marcel mumbled, "If you don't want to go to the prom with me, I understand."

"No! That's not it. My life is complicated right now," she responded.

"Oh, okay," he said with a look of disappointment.

With slumped shoulders, he turned around and walked away.

What? No, don't go, she thought.

She chased after him, tapped his shoulder, and said, "Wait, I didn't mean I don't want to go with you."

He turned around with a confused look on his face.

She bit her bottom lip and looked down at the floor, choosing her words carefully.

She couldn't tell him the truth, so instead she lied, "My grandpa said my curfew is at sunset."

"Sunset?" he asked, rubbing his forehead. "That's early. The party will be just getting started."

"Yeah, I know. I'll go to the prom with you if you can bring me home before eight thirty."

"Okay," Marcel said with a wide smile. "I can do that."

Cordelia's mood started to glow and her sadness diminished.

Finally, something good happened to me! She beamed.

~

At lunch, Cordelia brought her sandwich to the school library. She wanted to learn how fish navigated through water at night so she could understand her predicament and how to live with her condition.

"Do you have any books about marine animals and how they navigate through water?" Cordelia asked the librarian.

The woman searched the computer database and found a book about dolphins.

"The book is on the back wall near the water fountain," the librarian said.

"Thanks," Cordelia said.

After finding the book on the shelf, she sat down at a table. She learned how dolphins use sonar to navigate underwater by making clicking sounds with their nasal passages. The sound bounced off any hazardous obstacles in their path. According to the book, sound waves travel faster through water than in the air, which explained why her hearing was acute underwater.

Maybe I can make clicking sounds with my tongue, she thought.

~

Sitting next to the newly built aquarium, Cordelia admired the green evening gown in the full-length mirror. It was an old dress from her mom's closet that Cordelia modified for the prom. She had learned sewing and lace making from her mom. The dress sparkled with crystals, hugged her waist, and flared out from her knees down to her feet. She chose a dress that covered her legs and hid her scars, but more importantly, it made her feel beautiful.

Paula, the trapeze artist, stood behind Cordelia. The circus performers were back from Florida and soon they would be touring all over Michigan for the summer. Paula finished styling Cordelia's hair and helped apply her makeup. She added a crystal clip to

Cordelia's hair and stepped back, smiling with admiration.

"You look fabulous," Paula gushed. "Relax and have fun tonight. Leave your troubles behind, and enjoy the party."

"I'll try."

"If Marcel isn't a perfect gentleman, call me. Rego and I will come to your rescue," Paula offered. She often acted like Cordelia's older sister.

"I will," Cordelia replied. With a lump in her throat, she added, "I wish my mom was here to see me."

Paula wrapped her in a hug.

"Your mom was a good friend, and I miss her too," Paula whispered while rubbing Cordelia's back.

Cordelia heard a knock on the camper door.

"Come in!" she shouted.

Albert opened the door and gasped.

"Wow!" he exclaimed. "You look beautiful!"

Cordelia blushed as she bent down to strap her shoes.

"Marcel is here to pick you up."

She felt butterflies in her stomach.

Albert leaned in, kissed her forehead, and said, "Even though I don't think it's a good idea being out so close to sunset, I still want you to have a normal life. Be careful and watch the time."

~

Marcel and Cordelia sat in a local café with a casual atmosphere. They were surrounded by older couples sitting at their tables.

"Sorry I couldn't afford a nicer place," Marcel apologized as they ate their salads.

"No, it's fine. I like it here," she said before taking another bite.

He relaxed his shoulders as they continued their meal.

"What are your plans after high school?" Marcel asked.

"Umm…" Cordelia mumbled, looking down at the floor.

His question caught her off guard. All her aspirations were focused on the Olympics, but life as a mermaid limited her options. Life moved so fast. and she felt like she didn't have time to enjoy it.

"Maybe college," she replied. "What about you?"

"I'm still figuring it out," he responded.

"Me too," she said with a smile.

After dinner, they drove a short distance to the banquet hall for prom. Inside the hall, the music pulsated against the walls. She scanned the dark room for her friends. They waved and beckoned them to join their table.

Before they could sit down, the DJ played Cordelia's favorite song.

She grabbed Marcel by the elbow and said, "Come on."

Taken aback by her boldness, he let himself be guided to the dance floor. She tried not to giggle at Marcel's awkward dance moves. After a few quick songs, Cordelia pulled him back to the table so she could rest her knees.

"I'm having fun," Marcel said, holding Cordelia's hand and looking into her eyes.

Is he going to kiss me? she wondered as her heartbeat accelerated.

The lights dimmed, and the DJ played a slow song.

After a few awkward glances, he squeezed her hand and asked, "Would you like to dance again?"

She nodded, and a smile spread across her face. They glided onto the dance floor. Swaying to the music, Cordelia laid her head on Marcel's burly chest and lost herself in the moment. A tingling sensation ran through her legs and toes. Her throat turned dry when she noticed the clock on the wall read 8:20.

"We need to go," she insisted while trying to remain calm.

"Now?"

Cordelia nodded furiously. She tried running in her dress, but she tripped and fell to the dance floor. Several classmates stopped dancing and stared at Cordelia like a fish in a bowl. Ariel pointed at Cordelia and murmured amongst her friends. Panic flooded Cordelia's veins and her face turned bright red. She wanted to crawl under a seashell.

In shock, Marcel pointed at her feet. She looked down and saw her feet turning green.

"What's that?" he asked.

"I'm feeling sick," she made up an excuse.

He shook his head and said, "No, I mean what's happening to your feet. I'm taking you to the hospital."

"No, please take me home," she pleaded.

Marcel hesitated for a moment as his tough exterior slowly softened. He tilted his head sideways and stared deep into her eyes. After a brief moment, he gently picked her up in his arms. He carried her out of the banquet hall and into the parking lot.

Looking over Marcel's shoulder, she saw Coach John running toward them. He had been one of the teacher chaperones for the dance. He ran past them and stood in front of Marcel's car door.

"What's wrong with Cordelia?" Coach John asked.

"She feeling sick, so I'm taking her home," Marcel explained.

"She looks pale," Coach said. "We should take her to the hospital."

Cordelia shook her head and tried to speak, but she felt weak and dehydrated.

She leaned close to Marcel's ear and whispered, "Take me home. Now!"

"Coach, I can't take her to the hospital," Marcel persisted.

"Why not?" Coach asked sternly.

"Let's go," she whispered, gripping Marcel's shoulder.

Marcel pushed past Coach John, knocking him in the shoulder. John tumbled backwards and landed on the pavement with a thud.

"I'm so sorry," Marcel stammered with a frightened look on his face. "I didn't mean to knock you over. Sometimes, I don't know my own strength."

"You've changed," John said, slowly backing away from Marcel. "I don't know what's going on with you, but it scares me."

"It was an accident," Marcel tried to explain as Coach John scurried away.

Marcel opened the car door, gently placed Cordelia into her seat, and buckled her seatbelt. He slid into the driver's seat and sped off.

~

Gills opened up underneath her jawbones. Cordelia quickly covered them with her hands.

"What's going on?" Marcel freaked out and almost swerved off the road.

Fish scales protruded from her skin. Fearing for her life, she panicked.

"Get me home!" she cried in a scratchy voice.

The dashboard and headlights went dim. The car chugged and sputtered along the rural road.

"What's wrong?" she asked.

"I think the alternator is going out," he grunted.

The car rolled to a stop on the side of the road.

Marcel slammed his fist on the dashboard and spouted, "Stupid car!"

They were stranded several miles from her cabin.

"I'll get you home, hang on," Marcel said, jumping out of the car.

He popped open the trunk, pulled out his dumbbells, and pumped up his muscles, causing his pressed suit to rip. He groaned as he grew in size. The car rocked back and forth as he lifted up the front bumper. He dragged the car along the road, gaining speed with each passing minute.

She looked down at her watch; they ran out of time. Her legs slowly fused together, her lungs shut down, and her face turned blue. She faded out of consciousness.

29

~

"**Y**ou're home. What should I do now?" Marcel asked, nudging Cordelia's shoulder.

Choking for air, her eyes fluttered open.

She flailed her arms, pointed toward her RV, and sputtered, "My aquarium!"

Without asking questions, he quickly picked her up and carried her limp body into the camper. He lifted her above his shoulders and dropped her inside the aquarium. With her eyes closed, she plunged into the water. Feeling weightless and unable to move her muscles, she floated. Her brain sent signals to her limbs but her nerves weren't responding; her whole body felt numb.

Breathing through her gills helped calm her mind. Slowly, her heartbeat returned to normal, and her muscles regained strength. She opened her eyes.

Marcel stood in front of the tank, looking through the glass in disbelief. His jaw dropped as her fishtail burst through the seams of her dress. He stepped away from the glass and inched closer toward the door.

She had wanted to tell Marcel the truth, but she had been waiting for the right time. Now he knew. Before he could leave, she popped her head above the water and said, "It's okay. I'm a mermaid."

"That's impossible!" Marcel stammered. "How did that happen?"

"My grandpa tried to fix my legs with the scroll, but it turned me into a mermaid instead. It was an accident."

The camper door burst open, knocking Marcel in the arm.

Albert stepped inside the camper, ran up to the aquarium, and placed his hands on the glass.

Cordelia swam to him and leaned over the side.

"You're safe!" Albert exclaimed, letting out a sigh of relief. "I've been looking all over town for you."

He turned to Marcel and said, "Thank you for getting her home."

Still stunned by Cordelia's transformation, Marcel stared at Albert.

"You saved her life again!" Albert exclaimed. "How can I repay you?"

After Marcel regained his composure, he begged with desperation in his eyes. "Can you turn me back into a normal teenager? I can't become a weightlifter because they think I'm cheating."

"I'm sorry, but I can't change you back," Albert shook his head and apologized. "I tried reversing the spell on Cordelia, but it didn't work. Instead it turned her into a mermaid."

"I'll never become a professional bodybuilder," Marcel lowered his head and spoke with a sorrowful voice.

Deep in thought, Albert rubbed his chin.

"What if I hire you as a strongman for my circus?" Albert asked.

Marcel stepped back for a moment, turned his head, and looked into Cordelia's eyes.

"I would like that," Marcel responded.

Car headlights flashed against the windows of the RV. Albert glanced out the window.

"It's the police and your coach," Albert said. "What happened at the dance?"

"Marcel pushed our coach by accident," Cordelia explained. "He wanted to take me to the hospital, but I insisted on going home. Marcel didn't mean to push him so hard, but we were in hurry to get here."

"They must be here to check on your safety," Albert speculated.

"Oh no," Marcel groaned.

"Hide your tail while I stall them," Albert commanded.

"How?" Cordelia asked.

"I don't know, but you need to figure it out real soon!" Albert said.

30

~

Marcel paced the floor while Cordelia thought about how to hide her tail. The aquarium had tons of rocks and fish, but nothing was big enough to hide behind.

"Maybe I can carry you to the couch and put a blanket over you," Marcel speculated.

"I'll get sick if I'm out of the water too long," she stated.

Marcel continued to pace the floor.

"I know!" she exclaimed. "We can cover the front and sides of the aquarium with a blanket and sheets. They're in my dresser in my bedroom."

Marcel ran into the bedroom, grabbed the sheets, and draped them over the rim of the aquarium. He adjusted the height and width so the fabric covered the view of Cordelia's lower body.

Albert popped his head into the camper, "Cordelia, is everything okay? Can I come in?"

"Yes, come in," she replied.

Albert nonchalantly gave her the thumbs-up signal when he noticed the blankets covering the aquarium.

A police officer and Coach John stepped inside the RV. Their eyes widened when they saw the large aquarium filling the entire room.

"Wow!" Coach John exclaimed. "You have your own swimming pool?"

"Yes, we had it built this year," Albert responded.

"The reason we're here is to check on the wellbeing of your granddaughter," the officer explained in a formal tone. "Her coach said she fell at the dance. And then Marcel pushed John out of the way before they sped off."

"Cordelia forgot her pain medication for her knees," Albert tried to cover their tracks. "She was in a car accident last year and she still has pain."

"Yes, all the dancing flared up my pain," Cordelia chimed in. "That's why I fell during the dance—my knees were sore."

Looking at Marcel, the officer asked, "And why did push your coach?"

"I didn't mean to," Marcel explained. "I was in hurry to get Cordelia home, and I bumped into my coach. It was an accident."

"Well, it sounds like a misunderstanding," the officer stated. "John, do you want to press charges against Marcel?"

John thought for moment before answering, "No, that's okay."

"By the way, why are you in a pool?" the officer asked Cordelia.

"Floating in the water helps relieve my muscles, and I feel more relaxed," She responded honestly.

"Well, everything appears to be okay here," the officer added.

"Yes," John agreed with some skepticism.

The officer tilted his hat to Cordelia and apologized, "Sorry for the intrusion. We'll be on our way."

After they left, Albert let out a sigh of relief. "That was a close call."

~

Monday morning

As Albert drove her to school, Cordelia stared out the window and pondered how to explain the incident at the prom. Her friends would have a ton of questions about why she left early, and she didn't know how to respond.

Albert dropped her off at the main entrance, and she walked through the front doors.

Walking down the hall, Cordelia noticed several of her classmates staring at her. Some pointed, whispered, and giggled. It made her feel self-conscious.

Ariel leaned against Cordelia's locker with several girls from the swim team.

Oh great, now I have to talk to them, she thought.

As Cordelia approached her locker, one of the girls muttered under her breath, "Circus freak."

The hair on Cordelia's neck bristled, and her face turned bright red.

"Is it true?" Ariel asked a blistering question.

Cordelia braced herself and replied, "Is what true?"

"Why you left the prom early," Ariel spouted with glee.

Cordelia's lips turned dry and a knot formed in her stomach.

"I felt sick so I went home," Cordelia lied.

"That's not what I heard," Ariel continued. "Marcel said you turned into a mermaid."

Her whole world crashed down upon her. Her secret was exposed.

"Do you honestly believe you're a mermaid?" Ariel pressed her with questions.

The girls snickered. Cordelia shook her head and denied the rumor.

"Marcel was just kidding, and you fell for it," Cordelia shot back.

"You're crazy," Ariel said, rolling her eyes.

Holding back her tears, Cordelia felt vulnerable because Marcel betrayed her trust. She bitterly watched Ariel and her former swim teammates walk away.

With narrowed eyes and blood boiling, she stormed down the hall to Marcel's locker. When she rounded the corner, she saw Marcel throw his friend Kyle up against the locker. The boy slammed against the metal with a loud thud.

"I told you not to tell anyone!" Marcel shouted, pinning Kyle against the door.

"I thought you were joking around," Kyle stammered.

"Now she's never going to talk to me!" Marcel fired back.

"Sorry," Kyle meekly replied.

Coach John and another teacher ran out of their classrooms and broke up the fight.

"What's going on here?" Coach John asked as he stepped in between the boys and held up his hands.

"Kyle is spreading rumors," Marcel grunted.

"That's no reason to start a fight," Coach John scolded.

Coach John grabbed the two boys by the arms and led them to the principal's office. Marcel looked back at Cordelia with weary eyes. He mumbled something under his breath, but she couldn't make out his words.

31

~

June

*F*inally! *The last day of school,* Cordelia thought as she stood at her locker. She wanted to put high school behind her. She had become a social outcast; girls had continued to mock her, calling her a fake mermaid.

Marcel was suspended from school for fighting with Kyle. The principal put him on probation, so he could finish out his senior year. He avoided everyone in school. Instead, he focused all his time on his homework and graduating; Cordelia hadn't talked to him since prom.

Cordelia handed out invitations to her open house and hugged the few classmates who had stood by her side during her rough year. Her friends said they would come to her open house, but she couldn't tell if they were just saying that to being nice.

As she removed photographs from her locker, bittersweet memories of all her friends and teachers flooded her mind. When she found a photo from swim practice, a tear rolled down her cheek; it was a painful reminder of her failed attempt at making the Olympic swim team.

If I can't be in the Olympics, maybe I could go to college and learn how to design clothes like my mom, she pondered.

Her grandpa added her to the show, performing on the high dive platform. Her form was nowhere near the skill level before the accident, but she decided to tour with the circus over the summer which would give her time to think about what she wanted to study in college. The circus performers started asking questions about why Cordelia disappeared at night. Reluctantly, Cordelia told Paula, Rego, Sammy, and Buster her secret. Albert held a company meeting and asked everyone to keep the information private. Fortunately, everyone agreed to respect Cordelia's wishes.

Reflecting on the passing of her youth, she slung her backpack over her shoulder and meandered down the eerily quiet halls of the high school one last time. The world held so many possibilities that it almost frightened her. And then she remembered her limitations that came from being a mermaid.

Is it a handicap, blessing, or curse? she wondered. *Only time will tell.*

She pushed open the doors and the June sun warmed her skin. She saw Albert leaning against his truck. He smiled while opening the door for her. He started up the engine and pulled out of the parking lot.

"Congratulations!" he declared. "You've graduated. I'm so proud of you."

"Thank you," she responded with a half-smile.

Thoughts hung over her head like a cloud. On Mother's Day, Cordelia had visited her mom's grave and placed a white tulip on the headstone. The small gesture made her feel close to her mother. She didn't feel close to her dad. She hadn't seen him since the funeral.

Where is he? she pondered, staring out the window in silence.

"What's wrong?" Albert asked.

She let out a long sigh, put on a happy face, and muttered, "Nothing."

"Are you sure?"

"Yes," she responded.

"Wait until you see the tent for your open house," Albert said. "Everyone decorated for your party."

Unlike her friends, Cordelia's open house would be at the circus. She felt embarrassed by the location, but her grandpa had made all the arrangements and paid for the food.

~

The circus tent was filled with balloons and streamers. A giant banner with the word "Congratulations" written in bold letters hung on the back wall. Food, drinks, and a cake overloaded a long table.

Sammy created balloon animals while Buster performed tricks with his rodeo lasso. Paula and Rego swung on the trapeze bars while their two doves synchronized with their performance.

"Thank you, Grandpa," Cordelia said halfheartedly.

A few of her friends arrived for the party. She walked over to greet them and thank them for coming. Out of the corner of her eye, she saw Marcel enter the tent with a bundle of flowers.

She took a deep breath. *Do I really want to talk to him?* she asked herself.

"I'll be right back," Cordelia told her friends.

She stomped over to Marcel with her arms crossed and asked, "What are you doing here? You weren't invited."

"I'm sorry, Cordelia," Marcel responded with sincerity. "It was never my intention to hurt you. I told Kyle about what happened between us. I asked him to keep it a secret, but the story spread."

"It wasn't your secret to tell," she insisted, refusing to smile at him. "You ruined my senior year."

"I know. I'm sorry," Marcel said with sorrowful eyes. "It was a big mistake. I shouldn't have told Kyle. I trusted him."

"You should feel bad," she affirmed.

"Can you forgive me?" he begged.

She hesitated for a moment before replying, "Let me think about it."

Albert walked over to Marcel and looked him straight in the eyes with a dark stare.

"Hello, young man," Albert greeted him. "Thank you for saving my granddaughter, but you hurt her feelings. She told me about the rumors at school."

"I'm sorry. I came here to apologize," Marcel mumbled, lowering his head.

Albert relaxed his shoulders and looked at Cordelia. She nodded, acknowledging Marcel's honesty.

"Do you still have a job for me?" Marcel begged. "My parents told me I need a summer job, so I can pay them back."

"Pay them back?" Albert asked. "For what?"

"After I was disqualified from the Olympic competition, I was upset," Marcel confessed. "I went into the locker room and punched a few lockers. My parents paid for the damages, but my dad said I need to find a job and repay my debt, so I would learn my lesson."

"Nothing in life is free," Albert replied. "You need to control your anger if you want to work for me."

"I will," Marcel promised. "Can I still join your circus?"

"If it's okay with Cordelia, I think I can arrange that," Albert said, rubbing his chin.

Cordelia shrugged her shoulders. Her anger lingered in the air.

He apologized, and it did seem sincere, but... can I trust him? Can Grandpa trust him? she wondered.

Marcel shifted into a less defensive stance and scratched his head.

"What would I do, and how much do you pay?" Marcel asked.

"We can come up with a strongman act in our show. I'll pay you three-hundred dollars per week, plus free room and board," Albert explained. "Do you accept the deal?"

Looking a little nervous, Marcel shook Albert's hand and muttered, "Yes, but I hope I'm making the right decision."

Cordelia could relate to Marcel's anxiety toward the future. Life can changed by one single decision, for better or for worse. She was cursed to be a mermaid at night, but she tried to make the best out of the situation. Maybe Marcel could too.

～

The tent became strangely quiet after all the guests left the party. Albert turned off all the lights in the tent and walked out of the main entrance with Cordelia.

Placing his arm around her shoulder, he said, "I'm proud of you."

His words lifted her spirits, making her smile.

"Thanks, Grandpa," she said with a warm feeling in her heart.

An RV towing a livestock trailer pulled into the field and parked behind Albert's truck. Emotions and tears sprang up from within Cordelia's soul when her dad emerged from the vehicle.

32

~

Without hesitation, Cordelia ran into Salvatore's arms. She nearly knocked him over as she wrapped her arms around him. After a long pause, he lightly patted her on the back with his hand. Her heart sank when the hug felt hollow, devoid of any real emotion.

My Dad is back, but for how long? Has he changed for the better?

Salvatore reached into his pocket, pulled out a small gift-wrapped box, and handed it to Cordelia.

"I brought you a graduation gift. Congratulations."

She unwrapped the present, pulled out a tarnished gold locket, and opened it. One side of the locket had a picture of Albert who looked younger with tan hair and no wrinkles, and the other photograph was of her mom and dad standing together holding Cordelia when she was a baby.

"It's beautiful," she whispered, fastening the locket around her neck. "Thank you."

"You're welcome," Salvatore said gruffly. "It was your mother's necklace."

Albert's eyes narrowed as he sternly stepped forward to greet his son. His face turned bright red, and he breathed through his nose like a wild bull.

"So, my prodigal son has returned," Albert grunted. "I was wondering if you were ever coming back."

"I was in a bad place. and I needed to clear my head."

"You could've done that here, with us," Albert responded, stomping his foot.

Pointing to his RV, Salvatore explained, "I needed to get back on my feet, emotionally and financially."

"It looks like you're doing well for yourself," Albert firmly replied. "But you weren't here to help Cordelia through the hardest year of her life."

"I'm really sorry for that," Salvatore apologized.

Cordelia couldn't tell if he was being genuine, but it felt good to hear her dad apologize, either way.

"You think you can walk in here and pretend nothing happened? What if things get tough? Are you going to run away again?" Albert pressed.

"I believe I'm a changed person. I want to make things right."

"I'm warning you," Albert said, crossing his arms and tilting his head to the side. "You can't break Cordelia's heart again!"

Salvatore straightened his posture, raised his shoulders, and said, "I won't."

"Promise?" Albert demanded.

"I promise," Salvatore said.

Cordelia guarded her heart even though she was happy to see her father. He would have to regain her trust. She loved him, but her emotions were cluttered with resentment.

A tall man with a brown fedora and tan cargo pants emerged from her dad's camper.

"Who did you bring with you?" Albert asked.

"Jack is an old friend and college roommate," Salvatore replied. "After I left, I stayed at his house. He helped me through a difficult time."

"I see," Albert said, rubbing his chin.

"Besides, Jack used to work at the John Ball Zoo in Grand Rapids as an animal trainer," Salvatore said. "I figured we could use someone who has experience with animals. He would be a great asset to our circus."

"I already hired former rodeo clowns. They work with the animals," Albert explained.

"Rodeo clowns? They have experience with horses and bulls," Salvatore chuckled. "Jack has experience with all kinds of animals. And he has connections to buy exotic animals like lions and tigers. He brings a lot to the table."

Cordelia walked over to the trailer, stood on her tippy toes, and peered inside the window. A white rhino grunted and stomped around in the back of the trailer.

"Why did you bring a rhinoceros?" Cordelia asked, quite puzzled. "A circus should have elephants."

"Why should we be like everyone else?" Salvatore asked defensively.

"It's late," Albert interjected. "We'll talk about this another time." Turning to Cordelia, he continued, "It's almost sunset; you better go."

She let out a sigh. She felt nervous at the thought of telling her father about the curse, but she had to get it over with sooner or later.

How will my dad react? she wondered.

"Dad, could you come to my trailer please?" she asked with a trembling voice. "I need to show you something important."

"Sure," Salvatore replied.

She escorted him to her RV and opened the door. His eyes popped when he saw the large aquarium.

"What is this?" Salvatore asked.

"We built it so I can swim in privacy," she replied.

"But why?" he asked with a perplexed look.

"Let me show you."

She nervously went inside the bathroom and changed into the swimsuit made by her mother. Cordelia had customized the suit to fit her mermaid body. It looked more like a short dress that hugged her body rather than a bathing suit. When she emerged from the bathroom, she climbed inside the tank. As the sun began to set, her legs fused together, and fish scales protruded from her skin.

"What's happening?" Salvatore stammered, stumbling backward.

"It's because of the Secret Talent Scroll. During the day I walk

126

on land, and at dusk I turn into a mermaid."

She dove underwater and did a somersault. She flipped her tail, making a splash. Popping her head above the water, she said, "This is who I am now."

"Wow!" Salvatore exclaimed with a gleam in his eye. "Maybe you could be part of the show?"

Cordelia clenched her teeth.

"No way!" she bitterly replied.

"Hear me out," he suggested. "Instead of college, you could make a lot of money here."

"Why are you always thinking about money instead of me and how I feel?" she angrily asked.

Wondering what his true motives were for her and the circus, she crossed her arms and narrowed her eyes.

"Because I never had any money when I was growing up," he blurted out with a hint of honesty in his voice. "You deserve more in life."

Cordelia let out a scoffing noise as her shoulder muscles tightened.

"You should think about it," he suggested.

His eyes stared off into space as though he was scheming something in his head.

"Good night," Salvatore said, hurrying out the door.

Cordelia swam back and forth in the aquarium, pondering her dad's idea and her options for the future.

The crystal ball showed my dad coming home. Does this mean I'll swim in the Olympics too? How can I go to the Olympics or college if I'm a mermaid? Am I stuck in the circus forever? she wondered.

33

~

September

Salvatore and Cordelia sat around the kitchen table counting the money from the ticket sales while Albert nodded off.

"I need to lie down," Albert announced.

"Go ahead, I'll finish up here," Salvatore said.

With sleepy eyes, Albert lay down on the couch in the tiny living room.

"Son, all of your new ideas have helped double our ticket sales," Albert mumbled. "Especially since you made Marcel our featured performer. Great job!"

It was the first time Cordelia heard her grandpa give her dad a compliment. For a brief moment Salvatore's eyes shimmered, but that vanished, turning opaque once again.

"Thank you," Salvatore replied.

"Soon, you can take over the circus, so I can retire," Albert said.

Salvatore seemed a little surprised by his words.

"I can be in charge?" Salvatore asked.

"Yes, someday you'll be the boss," Albert said.

"I have more ideas on how we can improve the show," Salvatore said.

"Like what?" Albert asked.

"With a little help from the Secret Talent Scroll, we could give Paula and Rego the ability to fly during the trapeze act. And Sammy and Buster could have magic lassos. People from all around the world would pay to see them."

"Nonsense," Albert said with skepticism. "The scroll's powers can be used for good or bad. We shouldn't jump into things without thinking."

"Come on," Salvatore prodded. "We need to do this for our business. We could make a lot of money."

Cordelia squirmed in her chair, feeling uneasy about her dad's idea.

"It can't always be about the money," Albert responded.

"You think giving our employees magical powers is a bad thing?" Salvatore asked sternly.

"Yes, it can lead to bad consequences if it falls into the wrong hands," Albert said with a yawn. "I'm tired, let's talk about it later."

Salvatore grunted.

"Oh, before I forget," Albert said. "In the morning, I'm going to the next town for supplies and groceries. I'm also putting up posters for our next show. I'll be gone for a day or two."

"Okay," Salvatore mumbled.

Before Cordelia could express her concerns, she looked out the camper window. The sun had sunk low in the sky.

"I have to go," she interrupted their conversation.

She stood up and excused herself from the table. As she hurried out of her grandpa's camper, she bumped into Marcel.

"Hey," she responded, giving him a startled look. "You did a great job on your performance!"

"Thanks, it was a sold-out show."

"Wow! That's pretty good."

"Sort of," Marcel replied remorsefully.

"What do you mean?" she asked.

"People stare at me," Marcel explained. "They're scared of the size."

"I'm not scared of you," Cordelia replied.

Marcel smiled.

Noticing a rip in his t-shirt, Cordelia asked, "What happened?"

"Every time I perform, my muscles rip apart my clothes,"

Marcel groaned. "I have to be careful, the more I work out the bigger I get. After a while I shrink back to my normal size."

"I have sewing supplies in my trailer," she said. "I can put some elastic gussets in your clothes so the fabric can expand and contract with your muscles."

"Good idea!"

A random thought popped into her head.

"I have some new fish in my aquarium. Do you want to check them out while I sew your shirt?"

"Sure!" he replied with a smile.

~

Cordelia changed into her mermaid bathing suit, and then she sat down in front of her sewing machine.

"There's a robe in there," she suggested, pointing to the closet. "You can change in the bathroom while I fix your clothes. I have a little time before sunset."

"Okay, thanks," Marcel replied.

After a few minutes, he emerged from the bathroom and handed his clothes to Cordelia. She opened the drawer under the sewing table and pulled out some wide elastic.

"You have a lot of fish!" he said, pointing to the aquarium. "That's pretty cool!"

"Thanks," she replied while altering his clothes. "I've been collecting clownfish, lionfish, and blue lace fish."

"Where did you find the blue stones?"

"Those are called Leelanau Blues," Cordelia replied. "Every time we're in a city with a lake, I find new stones for my aquarium."

"Is that Viktor's key?" Marcel asked, looking at the bottom of the tank.

"Yeah," she replied. "I threw it in the tank."

She proceeded to tell him the story of how Viktor found the scroll during World War II and how a lightning bolt sank the *L.C. Woodruff*.

"And that's where I found the scroll, inside the sunken ship at the bottom of Lake Michigan," Cordelia finished the story.

"Wow!" Marcel exclaimed.

"At least Viktor is in jail now," she added, feeling more comfortable around Marcel. "Your show is popular with the crowds."

"I feel like a celebrity. But everyone keeps asking me how I got so big."

"What did you tell them?" she asked while nodding.

"I can't tell them the truth. Who would believe me anyway?"

"Yeah, you're right," she replied.

"I wish things were different," he said with a sigh. "I wish we were competing in the Olympics."

She realized they were in the same situation. They were outcasts in a traveling circus, but then she remembered how he betrayed her trust by telling her secret at school. However, she now felt less bitter about his mistake, and she felt sorry for him.

"I understand," she responded.

"Why can't the scroll change us back to normal?" he asked.

She stopped sewing for a moment and looked over at Marcel.

"The scroll has two spells," she said. "One gives you magic powers and the second chant reverses the spell but only if you use the powers for evil."

"Maybe we should become the bad guys." he suggested with a chuckle.

"Are you serious?" she asked and laughed.

"No," he said with a wink. "I'm just kidding."

"Or maybe my destiny was to become a mermaid," she said. "My grandpa keeps telling me to find my life's purpose using my talents, but this doesn't feel like a gift. It feels like a curse. I wish I knew what my life's purpose is supposed to be."

"I don't know what the future holds for us," he said, leaning in closer. "But I do know that I want to spend more time with you."

He leaned forward and kissed her. Caught off guard, she pushed him away. He was being aggressive, causing her heart and mind to race. She liked him, but she still hadn't completely forgiven him for prom and she wasn't ready for a kiss.

"What are you doing?" she cried.

"What's wrong?" Marcel stammered. "I thought you wanted me to kiss you."

Feeling her legs tingle, she leaned sideways with a million thoughts swirling in her head. She didn't know what to say or do, so she climbed up the ladder to the aquarium, slid into the tank, and swam to the bottom. Her legs fused together and gills opened under her chin. Feeling alone, she turned around, floated for a few moments, and stared through the glass at Marcel.

"Cordelia..." Marcel stammered. "I'm sorry! I thought that's what you wanted me to do."

Cordelia turned her head to the side and looked away.

"Fine," Marcel said and walked out the door.

Cordelia swam to the glass and placed her fingertips on the surface.

34

〜

The next morning, heavy thoughts swirled around in Cordelia's mind. She walked over to her grandpa's camper. She wanted to talk to him about her problems before he left. She knocked on the door, but he didn't answer.

Out of the corner of her eye she saw her dad and Jack carrying a giant banner that read, "Straight from the Ocean, Come See Cordelia, the MERMAID!"

She stormed over to them.

"What is that?" she yelled, pointing to the banner.

"We're putting up a sign over your new tent," Salvatore replied. "You'll have your own show as a mermaid."

"What?!" she asked angrily. "I don't want anyone outside of the circus to find out my secret!"

"Cordelia, embrace your true self," Salvatore insisted, pointing toward her legs. "Don't hide it, show the world!"

She crossed her arms, scowled at her dad, and asked, "How could you put me in a sideshow?"

"Sweetie, you'll make tons of money. You and Marcel deserve to be rewarded for your talents. Come on, let's check out your new tent."

Cordelia frowned and reluctantly followed him to the tent. Jack climbed up a ladder and hung the sign over the entrance.

Once the banner was level, Salvatore stepped back and exclaimed, "Perfect!"

They stepped inside the tent. As Cordelia's eyes slowly adjusted to the dim light, she saw the pool her grandpa had bought for her. The walls were cut down to three feet, and in the middle of the pool were a few prop boulders and a wooden platform.

"Where did the diving board go?" Cordelia grumbled.

"I got rid of it," Salvatore replied.

"Why? My circus act was jumping off the high dive platform."

"Not anymore. This is a better idea," he stated. "I lowered the walls of the pool so the audience can see you as a mermaid at night. You can swim around the pool or sit on top of the platform. We'll sell tickets outside."

"How could you do this to me?"

Bursting into tears, she ran out of the tent, climbed inside her camper, and slammed the door behind her. Pacing the floor, she contemplated her predicament.

I wish I could run away, swim in Lake Michigan at night, and live on the beach during the day. When Grandpa gets back, he'll help me fix things.

~

A few hours passed and her grandpa still hadn't returned. Instead of going stir-crazy in her camper, Cordelia helped Paula and Rego set up the trapeze equipment before the evening show. While they attached the safety net under the trapeze platform, Cordelia carried crates with supplies to the center stage. Her thoughts were a jumbled mess as she stared at the ground, avoiding eye contact with everyone.

Paula stopped working for a moment and asked, "Is everything okay? You've been quiet all day."

"I'm okay," Cordelia lied, biting her bottom lip.

"You can always talk to us," Paula said softly.

Should I tell her about my dad? Cordelia pondered her words for a moment. *Maybe she could give me some advice about Marcel too?*

Cordelia tripped, dropping the crate full of safety harnesses. Embarrassed, she kicked the crate and then dropped to her knees. She covered her face and cried. Paula ran over to Cordelia, leaned down, and placed her hand on her shoulder.

"What's wrong?" Paula asked.

"Can we talk in private?" Cordelia asked with tears rolling down her cheeks.

"Of course," Paula replied. "We can go to the dressing room in the back of the tent."

~

Letting her fingers run through the clothes, Cordelia could smell the musty fabric of all of the costumes made by her mom over the years. She stopped for a moment when she found Grandpa Albert's Fortune Teller's robe. She picked up the sleeve and squeezed it tightly.

"Have a seat," Paula said, pointing to the bench in front of the lockers.

Cordelia nodded as they sat down.

"What's wrong?" Paula asked.

Staring at the floor, Cordelia was at a loss for words.

"It's okay, you can trust me," Paula reassured her.

Suddenly all the emotions that had built up over the last year overflowed. Cordelia blurted out what happened with Marcel at school and in her camper.

Cordelia ended by saying, "Maybe Marcel was truly sorry. Maybe I should forgive him,"

"I would let your heart decide," Paula responded.

"And there's more," Cordelia added.

Cordelia talked about how her dad wanted to put her in the sideshow and how that would make her feel awkward and ashamed.

"That's terrible!" Paula exclaimed, shocked by the news. "I can't believe he wants to put you on display like that."

"What should I do?" Cordelia desperately asked.

"Everyone noticed your dad has changed since your mother passed," Paula responded with a worried look. "I wish I could fix things for you, but I'm not in charge."

After pouring her heart out, Cordelia felt a little better even though Paula couldn't provide any answers.

"Thanks for listening," Cordelia sighed.

Paula leaned in and hugged Cordelia.

"You can talk to me any time. My door is always open."

"Thank you," Cordelia replied.

"Your grandpa should be back soon," Paula said as she stood up. "He'll know what to do. I should get back to work so your dad doesn't get upset. If you need me, you know where to find me."

"Thanks, Paula."

~

Ducking out the back exit of the circus tent, Cordelia saw her dad sneaking into her grandpa's camper with Jack.

What are they doing? she wondered.

Curious, she crept up to the camper and peeked inside the window. While they rummaged through Albert's belongings, she listened to their conversation.

"We had a deal!" Jack grunted. "First we'll go city to city, then we'll head south and rob banks. Don't even think about erasing my memories. Without me, you'll never find what you're looking for."

"I'll get you the money I promised," Salvatore said. "But my dad keeps getting in the way."

"You should be in charge," Jack said.

"How would I do that?" Salvatore asked.

Jack's voice lowered as he spoke, "You can erase his memories so everyone will think he has Alzheimer's. He'll have no choice but to put you in charge."

Stunned by Jack's callous words, Cordelia angrily gritted her teeth.

"Here's a contract I made for the employees," Jack said, handing Salvatore some paperwork. "We'll be business partners and I'll help you manage the circus employees. We'll have two shows. The afternoon performance will be for the public and the evening show will be for the rich. A performance the world has never seen before!"

"Should we charge the public a higher price?" Salvatore asked, stuffing the contract into his coat pocket.

"Oh yes, they will pay. They'll pay us with their life savings."

Salvatore rifled through Albert's desk. Reaching into the bottom drawer, he pulled out the Secret Talent Scroll.

"Found it!"

As they shuffled toward the camper door, Cordelia hid behind the trailer.

"I'll tell everyone to meet you in the tent for a meeting," Jack said.

As Jack scurried off to assemble all of the circus performers, Cordelia quietly snuck into the main tent. She ducked underneath the bleachers and sat in the shadows, waiting to find out what Jack's true intentions were for the circus.

They're up to no good, she thought.

35

From under the bleachers, Cordelia watched the circus performers enter the tent, and they sat down on the bleachers in front of the center stage. She looked around for her grandfather, but he was nowhere to be seen. Normally he gave the pep talk before shows.

Carrying a bucket of water in one hand and Cordelia's rabbit cage in the other, Salvatore entered the tent. He was dressed sharply in a black suit with long coat tails, a top hat, and shiny black shoes. His mustache curled up in half circles at the tips, complementing his ringmaster outfit. He strutted to the center ring, stopped, and set the bucket and cage down on the ground.

What is my dad going to do with my rabbits? Cordelia wondered.

Salvatore lifted the microphone and announced, "I'm changing the show to appeal to a new generation."

The circus performers murmured and fidgeted.

"What kind of changes?" Buster nervously asked. Everyone's curious eyes were fixed on Salvatore as Buster spoke.

"I'm turning your circus talents into magical powers," Salvatore declared.

"What the heck are you talking about?" Sammy asked, rubbing his forehead. "Superpowers like in comic books?"

Everyone looked confused and their murmurs grew louder.

Has my dad lost his mind? Cordelia thought.

"I'll turn you into the best performers in the world!" Salvatore promised.

Buster spoke up again. "Does Albert know about this?"

"Yes, I've told him about my idea," Salvatore said angrily as his nostrils flared. "The circus will be more profitable. Who doesn't want to make more money?"

"Of course we all want to make more money, but how?" Buster asked. A few of the other performers nodded in agreement.

"I'll show you," Salvatore said with a devious smile. "Marcel, could you come to the stage with your dumbbells."

Marcel dutifully walked into the center ring, carrying his weights.

"Here's the future of our circus," Salvatore boasted. "Show them what you can do."

Looking nervous, Marcel curled the dumbbells. The more he curled, the bigger he grew until he stood 10 feet tall.

"Wow," Rego whispered. "How is that possible?"

Salvatore reached into his coat pocket and pulled out the Secret Talent Scroll. "Using the power of this scroll, I can turn you into the best circus performers in the world," Salvatore bragged. "You'll be famous."

Everyone grumbled.

"I don't think this is a good idea," Paula interjected. Her face expressed disbelief and concern. "I think Albert should be here so we can discuss this together. He's in charge of running the show."

Paula stood to leave, but Salvatore pulled out his pocket watch and raised it up to eye level. Like a magnet, all the performers became transfixed as they looked at the watch. Rotating his wrist back and forth, Salvatore hypnotized everyone. Their eyes glazed over, and their bodies froze in place like statues.

"I'm in charge of the circus now," Salvatore said with a strong voice. "As your new boss, you'll follow my directions."

What!? Cordelia thought. *How could my dad do this to them? To Grandpa!? I wish he was here!*

She wanted to run out of the tent and hide, but she stayed under the bleachers to gather more information so she could tell her grandfather later.

Like puppets, everyone stared at Salvatore without uttering a word as he put his watch back into his pocket.

"Paula and Rego, come to the center stage," Salvatore beckoned with his hand.

In a trance, the trapeze artists stiffly walked over to Salvatore. The trained doves swooped down from the trapeze ladder and landed on Paula and Rego's shoulders.

"I call upon the four classical elements: wind, fire, earth and water," Salvatore chanted. "Wind moves sand. Fire creates earth and ash. Earth absorbs water. Water quenches fire."

A tiny dust cloud spun around Paula and Rego. Their eyes widened, even under the trance they could register when something was happening to them. Their mouths opened as if to scream as the sand ignited into tiny sparks. Water sprang from the bucket and extinguished the sparks, turning the sand into ash. The ash fell on the doves' wings.

Salvatore ended the spell with the words, "Give Paula and Rego the ability to fly."

The birds' wings expanded to four feet long while their bodies disappeared. The wings fluttered in the air for a moment before attaching to Paula and Rego's shoulder blades, becoming like added limbs on their bodies.

"What have you done to us?" Paula asked in horror.

"In our circus, the trapeze artists fly!" Salvatore boasted. He let out a small evil laugh as Paula and Rego stared at their new wings in dismay.

"How long will this last?" Paula demanded. Her eyes were narrowed and looked like they could spit fire.

"I have given you a gift—be grateful," Salvatore responded.

Startled by his words, Rego moved to retaliate but Paula placed her hand on his arm. Instead, they both flapped their wings and lifted their bodies off the ground. Staring at each other in awe, they flew into the air and perched high on the trapeze platform.

Stunned, Cordelia stood frozen in place while a bead of sweat formed on her brow.

What in the world is he doing? Cordelia cried inside.

Turning his attention to Sammy and Buster, Salvatore rudely

asked, "Do you have any other talents besides being rodeo clowns?"

Still in shock, the clowns remained speechless.

"Well?" Salvatore demanded.

"We can make balloon animals," Buster stammered.

"That's it?" Salvatore asked. He thought for a moment and said, "Maybe we can combine your talents into one circus act."

Salvatore went backstage to the dressing room. When he returned, he carried two rolls of rope and a handful of balloons. He handed Buster and Sammy the props, who stared at the items in confusion. Salvatore chanted the words on the scroll.

A cloud of dust spun around the two clowns. The sand caught on fire, creating a mini fireworks show before a spout of water jumped from the bucket and extinguished the fire, turning the sand into ash. The ash fluttered onto the balloons and rope. The props dissolved into molecules and soaked into Sammy and Buster's skin. Their bodies turned into a rubbery plastic and expanded like balloons. They stretched their bodies into long lassos before contorting into different shapes and sizes. They awkwardly walked around, adjusting to their new form.

Paula and Rego stared at their friends from above, still baffled by the strange turn of events.

"Who's next?" Salvatore asked, pleased with himself.

Jack stepped forward, smiling, and rubbing his hands together.

Salvatore bent down, opened the rabbit cage, and handed Jack a white bunny.

"I saved the best for last," Salvatore said with sinister chuckle.

"Excellent. Thank you, my friend." Jack grinned with expectation.

"Since you're the animal trainer, I have something special for you," Salvatore bragged.

Salvatore read the scroll, and the dust cloud reappeared. The same events took place once again, and as the ash fell upon the rabbit, Salvatore demanded, "Give Jack the power to transform animals from one species into another!"

Jack set the rabbit down on the ground and petted its fur. The fur turned light brown, his fluffy feet sprouted claws, and his teeth became fangs. The rabbit morphed into a full-sized lion. The lion turned its head toward Salvatore and roared. Before it could take another step, Salvatore held up his pocket watch and froze the lion in place like a prize in a trophy room.

Nixie! Cordelia became upset. *My rabbit is gone!*

"Now that I gave everyone magical powers, we'll create the best circus performance in the world!" Salvatore exclaimed with a smug grin. He held up contracts and puffed out his chest. "However, I didn't give you these gifts for free. You'll pay back your debt to me by working in the circus for two years. If you refuse to sign this contract, I'll keep you frozen in time and erase your memories until you comply!"

The performers didn't ask for these powers, but Salvatore backed them into a corner with no way out. With fear in their eyes, they signed the contract.

Shocked by her father's actions, Cordelia couldn't bear to watch another minute. As she scurried out of the tent, she heard her father's voice bellow behind her, "Cordelia, come back here!"

36

~

With slumped shoulders, Cordelia took a big breath and walked back into the tent.

"Were you hiding under the bleachers?" Salvatore sternly asked.

"Yes, Father," she said with a lump in her throat.

Before she turned away, he raised the pocket watch to eye level and hypnotized her. She became fixated on the watch.

"You will keep an open mind about being a mermaid in the circus," Salvatore said in a monotone voice. "And you will do as I say."

While standing frozen like a statue, Cordelia heard Jack say, "You always manage to amaze me with that watch. How do you do it?"

"I learned to fast-forward, stop, and erase time. Memories are the stories we tell ourselves. And if memories are created over time, I can use the watch to erase them," Salvatore explained. "I figured out how to manipulate people."

"Wow!" Jack exclaimed.

Salvatore snapped his fingers.

"It's time for your show," Salvatore announced, placing his top hat on his head.

Cordelia tried to raise her arms in protest, but she felt a heavy gravitational pull on her arms and legs. She felt trapped in one moment in time. She could see, hear, and speak, but she couldn't move her body.

"Maybe this is your true destiny," Salvatore speculated, raising his eyebrows. "You have a lot to offer this world."

Her face turned red. She never defied her father before, but today she had a lot to say.

Before she could reply, Salvatore held up the pocket watch and gave his spiel. "Come with me. Together, we can rule the circus!"

As though guided by an invisible force, she followed Salvatore to her new tent. As the sun began to set, she climbed into the pool while Jack stood outside the tent collecting money.

Swimming underwater and breathing through her gills, she heard the sound of shuffling feet and the murmuring of a crowd. She popped herself above the water and crawled onto the platform. A crowd of spectators had gathered around the swimming pool.

Salvatore held a microphone up to his chin and announced, "Cordelia lives in two worlds—by day she walks on land, and by night she swims in Lake Michigan..."

The performance in front of a live audience became a blur.

~

After the crowd left her tent, Cordelia floated at the bottom of the swimming pool angrily pondering her lot in life. Feeling the hypnotizing power of the pocket watch slowly wear off, she felt betrayed. She tossed and turned in the water all night while negative thoughts swirled in her head.

~

In the morning, she barely remembered the show. Some parts of the evening were clear, but others parts were blurry. She felt conflicted about her part in the show. Her head told her to follow her dad's orders, but her gut told her not to listen to him.

As her fish tail disappeared, she climbed out of the pool, changed into dry clothes, and stepped outside in the fresh morning air.

The campground looked like a ghost town. Usually all of the circus employees were busy starting the carnival rides and preparing for the circus performances.

Where is everybody? Cordelia wondered.

Remembering Paula's invitation to talk anytime, Cordelia walked over to her camper and knocked on the door. Feet shuffled behind the door.

"Who is it?" Paula asked without opening the door.

"It's Cordelia."

Paula slowly opened the door a sliver and nervously looked around the campground.

"Are you alone?" Paula asked.

"Yes," Cordelia responded.

"Okay," Paula waved her in.

Cordelia stepped inside. Rego, Marcel, Sammy, Buster, and few other employees were crammed in the tiny camper. They all looked nervous and afraid.

"What is going on?" Cordelia asked.

Paula handed Cordelia some paperwork.

"Your father told us he would erase our memory if we don't follow his orders," Paula said in a trembling voice.

Cordelia read the contract:

You are required to work for Salvatore Da Vinci for no less than two years. The circus will receive a portion of your profits until you repay your debts to Salvatore for receiving these special skills.

"We're scared of your dad," Paula added.

"We're trying to figure out what to do next," Rego explained.

Cordelia tensed when she heard a knock on the door. Paula peered out the window.

"It's Jack, we better get back to work before Salvatore gets upset." Paula said.

As everyone exited the camper, Jack had a perplexed look on his face.

"What's going on?" Jack asked.

Paula sheepishly looked at Rego.

Oh no! Jack is suspicious, Cordelia thought.

"Oh, nothing," Rego lied. "We were just talking about our new talents."

"Well, you better not be planning your escape because Salvatore could erase your memories just like that," Jack warned, snapping his fingers.

"He would do that?" Paula asked with fear in her eyes.

"Yes," Jack replied, pointing at all the circus employees. "He could use the power of his pocket watch to erase all your memories. Imagine waking up, learning everything all over again. And don't even think of going to the police. Salvatore can control time and space with his watch."

Cordelia flinched at his callous tone as the employees cringed in fear.

"Salvatore is waiting. Let's get to work" Jack commanded.

Cordelia nervously nodded along with everyone else. They went about their daily routine, waiting for Albert's return.

I need to warn Grandpa! I'm sure he'll fix everything, Cordelia hoped.

37

~

Thirty minutes before sunset, Cordelia glanced out her camper window and noticed light emitting from inside the circus tent.

What is going on? she thought as she stepped outside her camper to investigate. *The last circus performance ended at 7:30 pm.*

The carnival-goers had gone home and the circus performers were nowhere to be seen, though circus music echoed through the empty park.

Feeling a tap on her shoulder, Cordelia nearly jumped out of her skin. She turned around and saw Albert holding two bags of groceries.

"You're back!" she said with a sigh of relief.

"I wasn't gone that long," Albert responded with a chuckle. After he set the grocery bags down on the ground, she gave him a big hug.

From inside the tent, Salvatore announced over the loud speaker, "For the first act we have Paula and Rego, the trapeze artists!"

"What's going on?" Albert asked.

"Dad took over the circus!" Cordelia exclaimed.

"What?" Albert asked, marching toward the tent.

Cordelia chased after him, leaving the grocery bags behind.

Inside the tent, a single family sat in the bleachers while Salvatore stood in the center ring with a microphone.

"I call their performance 'Sky Circus,'" Salvatore bragged.

A spotlight focused on Paula and Rego standing on a trapeze platform high in the air. On Salvatore's cue, they jumped off the platform in unison.

"Where are the safety nets?" Albert asked.

Cordelia shrugged her shoulders.

Before hitting the ground, white wings sprang from Paula and Rego's shoulder blades. They flew up into the air, brushing their hair on the ceiling of the tent.

Cordelia stopped in her tracks, transfixed by the show.

"That's impossible!" Albert exclaimed.

The spotlight swept across the floor and landed on Marcel, Sammy, and Buster in the center ring. Marcel stood 12 feet tall. He had lifted the rhinoceros from the ground. Sammy and Buster had stretched out their bodies like balloons.

"How did this happen?" Albert asked Cordelia.

"Dad used the scroll on them," she responded.

Albert scowled, marched into the main ring, waved his hands in the air, and stopped the show.

"What is going on?" Albert sternly asked.

"We're putting on a private show for the Rockefeller family," Salvatore said, gesturing toward the bleachers.

Richly dressed, the Rockefellers sat transfixed as though they were statues in a museum. An open briefcase, containing wads of cash and jewelry, sat on the bench seat in front of the family.

Is my dad controlling them with his pocket watch? Dozens of questions ran through her mind.

"I didn't say you could change the show," Albert insisted. "And you can't use the scroll behind my back!"

"Relax, no one got hurt," Salvatore said.

"Not yet," Albert grunted.

"This is the future! Don't you want to own the best circus in the world?" Salvatore asked. Pointing to the briefcase, he continued, "Look at how much I made from one show."

Albert's eyes widened when he saw the piles of money inside the briefcase. And then he looked up at the family who were frozen in time.

"Imagine what we could make for the whole year," Salvatore said with a glimmer in his eye.

"Whatever is going on, I don't like it," Albert snapped back.

"You're just mad because I made more money with the circus than you."

"Did they pay for the show, or did you steal it from them using your pocket watch?" Albert demanded with fury in his eyes.

"How dare you accuse me of stealing?" Salvatore shouted, his face turning red. "Why can't you trust your own son to run the circus?"

"Because you've changed," Albert stammered. "Besides, I'm still in charge."

"Not anymore. If you can't see the future, I have no choice but to take over the circus."

"What do you mean?" Albert asked, raising his eyebrows.

"You don't have a choice," Salvatore shot back.

"What?" Albert asked.

Cordelia watched in horror as her father lifted his pocket watch and swung it back and forth.

"Erase Albert's memories from tonight," Salvatore spoke to the pocket watch.

Drifting into a trance, Albert wobbled for a moment before dropping to his knees. He rubbed his forehead with both of his hands, and his eyes glossed over.

"Dad, what have you done?" Cordelia demanded, running to Albert's side.

Salvatore grabbed the briefcase in the bleachers and handed it to Jack.

"Take it to my trailer," Salvatore instructed.

Jack nodded.

Standing in front of the Rockefeller family, Salvatore snapped his fingers. Looking confused, they awakened from their slumber.

"The show is over," Salvatore stated coldly. "It's time to go home."

The family staggered out of the main tent.

Looking at the circus performers, Salvatore yelled, "Pack your bags. We're heading to the next town!"

Everyone picked up their equipment and dismantled the tents as Albert stared off into space, dazed and confused.

"You're not leaving Grandpa here!" Cordelia exclaimed.

Pointing to Marcel, Salvatore commanded, "Take her away!"

Marcel flinched at his words.

"Marcel, you're the strongest person in the world," Cordelia pleaded. "You can stop him!"

Marcel straightened his shoulders, flexed his muscles, and charged Salvatore.

"You're making a big mistake!" Salvatore shouted. He held up his pocket watch and swung it back and forth.

Mid-run, Marcel froze in place. With panic in his eyes, he struggled to break free from the trance, but the alteration of time and space overpowered his muscles.

"No!" Cordelia yelled.

Salvatore strutted over to Marcel and looked deep into his eyes.

"You're a brave young man, but you left me no choice. I'm going to erase all your memories," Salvatore snickered. "Imagine learning how to walk and talk all over again."

Marcel's cheeks and eyes reddened with anger.

Cordelia ran in between the two men, held up her hands, and said, "Dad! Stop! Don't do this to him."

"Why?" Salvatore asked.

Looking down at the ground, Cordelia said, "Because I care about him."

Salvatore's face softened a bit. He looked at Marcel and then back at Cordelia.

"He could be useful," Salvatore muttered, rubbing his chin. "He could keep everyone in line."

Oh no! Cordelia feared.

"Will you follow my orders?" Salvatore asked, pointing his finger in Marcel's face. "Blink your eyes twice, if you agree."

Marcel blinked his eyes.

"Good," Salvatore said as he released Marcel from the trance. "Take her away!"

With regret in his eyes, Marcel picked up Cordelia and slung her over his shoulder. As he carried Cordelia back toward her RV, she pounded her fists on his back.

"Marcel, put me down!" she shouted.

He continued walking despite her protests. "I'm sorry, Cordelia."

Marcel kicked open the camper door, stepped inside, and gently set her down on the couch.

"Can you stop him?" she pleaded as her fingers gripped the seat cushions.

"I felt the power of your dad's watch," Marcel said with a look of fear. "I'm scared!"

Before she could respond, her father marched into the RV.

Salvatore turned to Marcel and said, "Do you want to compete in the Olympics someday?"

Marcel glanced at Cordelia with a furrowed brow and nodded.

"Do what I say and I'll make that happen," Salvatore said. "I need to talk to my daughter alone. Wait outside."

Lowering his head and dropping his shoulders, Marcel left them alone.

Salvatore sat down on the couch next to Cordelia and placed his hand on her shoulder. His warmth faded, and his gentle touch turned cold. Frightened, she backed away from her dad.

"What is going on?" she asked with a quivering lip and a knot in her stomach.

"Let me explain," he replied.

He held up the pocket watch and swung it back and forth. Cordelia tried to resist looking, but the watch pulled her eyes to it like a magnet. Leaning back against the couch, she became transfixed by the shiny object.

"You won't remember anything that happened tonight," Salvatore said in a monotone. "You won't remember being mad at me or your grandpa losing his memory. You'll listen to what I say and go along with the decisions I make moving forward."

All of the images in her mind were replaced with a sea of darkness. The last thing she remembered was Salvatore carrying her to her aquarium.

38

~

The sound of fabric curtains rustling together echoed through the small ear holes under Cordelia's jawbones. She awakened at the bottom of her pool as sunlight shimmered off the water's surface and air bubbles floated around her body. Her gills began to close and her lungs expanded. Hearing the phone ring, she swam to the surface, climbed out of the tank, and dried off.

"Hello," she said, holding the phone up to her ear.

"I'm calling on behalf of Albert Da Vinci," a male voice spoke on the other end. "I'm looking for his granddaughter, Cordelia."

"This is Cordelia," she replied. Her heart began to race, and she feared the worse.

"Your grandfather showed up late last night at Mercy Hospital. He appeared confused. He had your phone number in his wallet."

"Is he okay?"

"Yes. Could you or a family member come pick him up?"

"We'll be right there."

Cordelia asked the man for the address and jotted it down. She hung up the phone and ran outside. Suddenly she became disoriented. They were in a new campground and she couldn't remember how she got here. The previous night was a blur.

Who drove me here? she wondered.

Searching the campground, she found her dad near his RV, talking with Jack.

"Grandpa is in the hospital," she sputtered. "They called and said he showed up late last night. He's okay, and we need to pick him up."

Salvatore neither looked surprised by the news, nor did he flinch. He let out a long sigh and rolled his eyes.

"Aren't you worried? We need to talk to the doctor and find out what's wrong," she pleaded.

"Settle down," Salvatore insisted with a gruff voice. "Grandpa is getting older; maybe he belongs in a nursing home."

She crossed her arms and her face hardened.

"What? No way!" she refused to accept her dad's idea. "If you're not picking him up, I will," she insisted defiantly.

"Okay, fine," Salvatore reluctantly agreed. "I'll grab my keys. Meet me at my truck."

~

Cordelia angrily stared out the window while Salvatore drove into town.

How could he even suggest a nursing home for Grandpa? she thought.

"I'm sorry I was stern with you earlier," Salvatore apologized. "Since your mom passed, I've become numb toward the world."

She didn't acknowledge his apology or his honesty.

"I was wrong, and I messed up," Salvatore continued. "I hope you can forgive me."

He placed his hand on her shoulder. For a brief moment she felt warmth in his touch. She turned and looked at him.

"Do you know why I left?" he asked.

That question burned deep inside her. Her heart filled with a sudden rush of emotions. She felt as if that moment in time had screwed up all her decisions since.

"No! Why did you leave?" she yelled, letting out all her pent-up anger.

"I failed you and myself. I couldn't bring back your mother. And that's a burden I carry with me every day."

Holding back her tears, she punched the truck dashboard with her fist. It hurt her hand, but she didn't care.

"But I'm here now, and I want to make it up to you, but you have to trust me," he begged his daughter.

She took a deep breath and thought, *How could I trust him after everything he put me through?*

"I could give you everything you ever wanted, clothes, jewelry, and a new house," Salvatore promised. "We could have it all if we used the Secret Talent Scroll. You have a special gift as a mermaid. You deserve to be rewarded for your talents."

I work hard, and I have nothing to show for it. Maybe I should accept my fate as a mermaid, she contemplated.

"I also gave everyone at the circus special powers," Salvatore confessed. "I'm creating a circus performance the world has never seen before! People will pay us a ton of money to see the show."

"So this is all for money?" she asked. "I don't want money. I want my old life back."

Tightly gripping the steering wheel, Salvatore said, "I made a deal with Jack. I think I found a way to bring back your mom and help you overcome the mermaid curse so you can achieve your Olympic dreams."

Cordelia's jaw dropped and her face turned pale.

"How? What kind of deal?" Her dry voice crackled.

"I have a plan," Salvatore said. "But your grandfather would never go along with it"

"What is the plan?"

Keeping his eyes on the road, Salvatore stared straight ahead without saying a word.

"Tell me!" Cordelia shouted.

"No," Salvatore sternly said. "Bringing your mom back is too important."

Cordelia bit her bottom lip.

"I'll give you everything you desire, but you have to keep this a secret," he bargained. "I'll give you the world if you'll put your trust in me."

Cordelia pondered her dad's words. Keeping a secret from her grandfather caused a knot in her stomach. Something didn't feel right, but she couldn't put a finger on it. Without answering, she felt his words hang in the air like a dark storm cloud.

39

～

Cordelia sometimes had nightmares about the hospital. She felt stifled and confined by the sterile white walls of the tiny examining room at Mercy Hospital. She bit her bottom lip as they waited for the doctor to arrive.

Tapping his foot on the checkered tile floor, Salvatore squeezed his hands into a fist.

Albert looked around the room with a blank stare. His hair was uncombed and his chin unshaven. He looked a mess, and Cordelia worried about him.

A tall gentleman in a white coat entered the room, carrying a pen and clipboard.

"Hello, I'm Dr. Parker," he introduced himself and waved.

The doctor sat down in a chair on the opposite side of the small room. "I performed a few cognitive tests, and I ordered an MRI for Albert. Unfortunately, we determined he has the early signs of Alzheimer's and dementia."

This is why I hate hospitals, it's always bad news, Cordelia thought.

She looked over at her dad who seemed unfazed. Albert perked up and become more alert.

"I feel fine," Albert said, blinking his eyes. "I'm starting to remember things."

"Can you remember how you got here and what happened last

night?" the doctor asked.

"No, but I do remember walking here from an empty field," Albert said with a determined look on his face. He scowled at his son, "Why did you leave me behind?"

"You must've wandered off," Salvatore replied, squirming in his seat. "When we realized you were missing, we looked all over for you."

"It's starting to come back to me!" Albert suddenly spoke with clarity in his voice. "We had an argument and then... then I woke up in the middle of a field!"

"What are you talking about?" Salvatore said defensively. "We wouldn't leave you in a field? That's nonsense!"

Cordelia scowled. Even though she couldn't remember what had happened last night either, she couldn't tell if her dad was lying. Something in her heart didn't feel right.

Did Dad leave Grandpa behind? Cordelia wondered. *Has he gone too far? Can I even trust him?*

~

Upon returning to the campground, Cordelia noticed the circus performers packing all of their supplies into their campers.

"Where are we going?" Cordelia asked.

"We're heading to Whitehall and setting up in Funnell Field," Salvatore stated.

"I don't feel good," Albert said, rubbing his stomach.

"Okay," Salvatore replied. "Marcel can drive your camper so you can lie down."

Albert nodded.

"Cordelia, can you keep an eye on him?" Salvatore asked.

"Yes, Dad," Cordelia replied.

~

While Marcel drove the camper to Whitehall, Albert and Cordelia sat in the back where Marcel couldn't see them or hear their conversation.

Albert looked around nervously.

"Grandpa, what's wrong?" Cordelia asked anxiously.

He placed his index finger on his lips and whispered, "Shhhhh... Something bad is happening to our circus. I think your dad is behind it, but I don't have any proof. We need to find out how to stop him before it's too late."

He pulled out the crystal ball from his duffle bag and set it on the table. He placed his hands over the ball and waved them in a clockwise motion. Purple smoke swirled inside, revealing a tall, slender boy with blonde hair entering Cordelia's tent.

"Who's that?" she asked.

Cordelia became startled when a low voice emitted from the crystal ball, "Help this boy find his courage, and he will save the circus and help Cordelia compete in the Olympics again."

The voice sounded familiar, but Cordelia put her finger on it.

"What was that?" Cordelia asked, raising her eyebrows. "When did it start talking?"

"Just now," Albert said. His face turned pale and voice crackled. "This is the first time I've heard the crystal ball speak. It sounded just like your grandma Elsa, but it can't be her. That's impossible!"

"What should we do?" Cordelia asked, staring at the boy in the crystal ball.

Still shaken, Albert leaned back in his seat and remained deep in thought.

"I don't think we should push the boy into being courageous, he needs to find it on his own," Albert whispered. "Instead, let's guide and encourage the boy to become brave. You can't force someone to be something they're not."

Should I tell Grandpa the truth about Dad? Cordelia wondered.

"We should keep this a secret so your dad doesn't find out," Albert concluded.

"Okay," Cordelia reluctantly agreed.

No more secrets! she desperately thought.

She reflected on all the decisions that brought her to this moment. If she hadn't used the scroll, she wouldn't have won the

Olympic competition. And maybe she would've never been in a car accident, and her mother would still be alive. When her grandpa used the crystal ball, it led her to becoming a mermaid.

Why should I trust the crystal ball now? she thought.

She had a difficult decision to make. Trust her dad, or follow her grandpa.

～

Standing outside her tent and waiting for the sun to set, Cordelia saw a tall, skinny boy riding his bike on the outskirts of Funnell Field. He was a plain-looking boy but for some reason he caught her eye. Even from afar, she felt like she could sense his insecurity and shyness. It was the oddest thing to feel a connection with someone she was just looking at and knew nothing about.

Is that the boy from the crystal ball? she wondered. *Can he really change things?*

Her legs tingled and her breathing became heavy. She jumped into the swimming pool before turning into a mermaid.

～

A beam of light streamed from the center of the tent where a single bulb dangled below the canvas. A kid entered her tent. He looked like the boy from the crystal ball, but she wasn't sure. A line of customers stood elbow-to-elbow. A pile of boulders filled the center of the above-ground pool and the water surrounded Cordelia like a moat. She sat on top of the rocks, and her fish tail swayed back and forth in the water. Her curly hair cascaded over her shoulders, and her skin showed a hint of freckles.

Salvatore stood on a wooden barrel, held a microphone to his mouth, and gave his well-rehearsed pitch, "Witness the beautiful and coy Cordelia. She lives in two worlds—by day she walks on land, and by night she swims in the ocean. Cursed by a spell, her long legs turn into a fish tail at dusk, making her the fastest, prettiest creature in the sea. But beware! She'll seduce you into the water, and once

160

you immerse yourself, she'll pull you to the bottom and keep you there. I suggest you avoid prolonged eye contact, so look quickly and move on. Let everyone take a gander at this rare creature."

She knew it was show business, and her dad painted a fantasy world with his words, but the performance made her squirm uncomfortably.

Cordelia's bright green eyes scanned the faces in the audience. She made eye contact with the boy. She wanted a closer look at his face, so she smiled at him and beckoned him to come closer to the pool. He looked startled and responded with a meek smile.

Oh no, he probably thinks I'm a freak with a fish tail, Cordelia thought.

Her dad narrowed his eyes, looked straight at the boy, and said, "You better move on, kid. She likes you. And that can be dangerous."

To be continued...

Book 1:
Traveling Circus
And the Secret Talent Scroll

This book follows the adventures of Cordelia as she discovers the
mystery behind the Secret Talent Scroll.

Book 2:
Traveling Circus

The ringmaster, wielding a magic pocket watch that controls time,
holds Flynn against his will. Flynn must find his inner courage to
defeat the ringmaster and go home.

Book 3:
Traveling Circus
And the Skeleton Key

The conclusion to the Traveling Circus Series. Will Cordelia achieve
her Olympic dream or remain forever stuck in a circus sideshow?

Made in the USA
Monee, IL
10 May 2021